PUSH!

AN ANTHOLOGY OF CHILDBIRTH HORROR

EDITED BY RUTH ANNA EVANS

Contents

FOREWORD

Candace Nola

CHILDBIRTH. THAT SINGLE WORD conjures up a thousand images, does it not? Pain and joy, beauty and blood, fear and wonder, screaming faces, arched backs, spread legs, crowning heads covered in matted fuzzy hair. Genitals rent and raw and gushing fluids of all kinds. Nothing and no one can prepare a new mother for childbirth. Not a book, not a class, not a doctor, not a thousand other women telling her exactly what it was like…for them. And that is the kicker, is it not? *For. Them.*

No two women are alike and no two pregnancies or subsequent labor will be alike, not even within the same woman. Every experience is different based on myriad factors: her age, her weight, her mental state, her diet, her immune system, her body structure and hormonal balance at that precise moment. The list of factors is never-ending, as is the list of things that can and do go wrong every single day.

Did we mention the fear? The all-consuming fear of doing it wrong? Of eating the wrong thing, drinking the wrong thing, buying the wrong crib or the wrong car seat, feeding the baby wrong, dropping the baby, drowning the baby, shaking the baby, hating the baby, hating yourself, hating your partner. The fear of the baby dying, of the baby not surviving, of the baby being born critically ill, or of you dying right there on the delivery table? Fear, these fears, will consume you for the duration.

Oh, too much? I think not. These are all very real fears, thanks to the well-meaning advice of others, the expectations of society, of friends, of our partners. Not every woman has the maternal instinct, not every woman chooses to get pregnant or when, not every mother has a perfect biological clock that tells them when, and where, and how to raise a perfect child.

Take all of that, cram it into a nine-month long experience of sensory overload, exhaustion, and mounting terror, and tell me how well you think you will do when the time comes. When your stomach is so etched with stretch marks, you fear you might burst wide-open or when your breasts are so swollen, you cry from just putting a bra on. When your spine feels like it is breaking, when your pubic bones throb and ache, when your body tells you to push, to push like you never have before and you scream like you never knew you could.

This book is exactly like that. Nothing and no one, not even this introduction, can prepare you for what lies within, pregnant and pulsing and ready to be birthed into your world, shrieking and bloody. The stories told within explore every possible theme mentioned above and beyond, from WTF moments (looking at you, Marie LeStrange), to impossibly gut-wrenching (gestures at Paul Avery Tindol) and beyond bizarre (side-eyes S.E. Howard), PUSH is an anthology like no other.

Every single author in this anthology has brought you a special delivery. All you need to do is PUSH through your fear.

Candace Nola, author of Bishop and Demons in My Bloodstream.
Feb. 4, 2025.

INTRODUCTION

Ruth Anna Evans

I WANTED TO CREATE this book because pregnancy and childbirth truly are horror. Anticipated pain is one of the most frightening things there is. When you know your world is going to be rocked by unavoidable, overwhelming, all-consuming pain, you feel like a different person. A vulnerable person. A fragile person. Carrying a child is the constant anticipation of pain.

And then there's childbirth itself. You could fail. You could literally fail to push the baby into the world, and its head could get stuck in your pelvis, and its brain could get crushed and it could die. Its brain could get crushed and it could live. The pressure is unbelievable.

Even when everything goes right, it can be awful. You're trapped in a bed surrounded by people you don't know, pushing your insides out. Pain relief is unreliable. You shit. You scream. You feel like a wild animal. Your vagina rips. Sometimes they cut you to your asshole. And then they flop a baby on your chest.

There is joy, for most of us. The baby's black eyes staring at us with wonder. The absolutely precious fingers and toes. This while they are stitching up your vagina and hoping your placenta doesn't rip a chunk out of your womb and you bleed to death.

And for some, there is no joy. There is a cold bundle with blue lips and sadness that will never be wept away.

But if you bring home a baby, even when things are perfect, even when you have money for formula and working breasts, a supportive partner, a job that doesn't demand you back to work a week later. Even when you have what many do not, it can be horrible. The baby shits constantly, cries constantly, doesn't sleep, your arms are tired, your back is tired, and you don't have time to change your own diaper, which is supposed to cool your swollen, stitched vagina but barely helps.

Sometimes your mind breaks. You feel like throwing the baby down the stairs, or throwing yourself down the stairs. Doctors pat you on the hand and tell you to sleep when the baby sleeps, but the baby never fucking sleeps. It Never. Fucking. Sleeps.

And then there is this book. Which is way, way, worse than any of that. The authors whose stories I present to you here crystallized the fear and agony of becoming a parent and brought it to you in a disturbing, weird, and wonderful way. I'm so proud to share these stories with the world and I can't wait to hear what you think. That is, if you can stand the pain.

JUST LIKE A CERTAIN CHOCOLATE EGG TOY

Antonija Mežnarić

IF YOU ASKED ANDREA, there was nothing more humiliating than kneeling in front of the toilet, watching the splatter of green-brown mush on the ceramic and inhaling the pungent stench, while her throat constricted with the onslaught of last night's half-digested meal. This was her second time over the span of half an hour she'd had to run from her bed to the bathroom, this one worse than the last, her whole body shaking with the violent push to expel everything stored, liquid and firm. Another burst of vomit started passing through her, stopping at the crucial moment in her throat, choking her.

Something heavy stayed stuck, and in pure panic she clawed at her own neck, crying and heaving and suffocating, cursing out her husband who hadn't even stirred in his sleep while she was loudly throwing up. With another vicious contraction from her body, the sour clump dislodged from her throat and, in free fall, hit the toilet soup of her insides and water with a splash, spraying her chin and cheek. She was ready to collapse on the floor—cool her heated skin on the tiles, breathe in the welcome air even if sourness permeated it, enjoy the moment of respite—when she saw what had come out of her.

In her stomach waste, floating amidst green beans and other squashed fragments of her dinner, were five little fingers attached to a small palm.

At least she now knew that her shocked scream would definitely bring her husband running to her. Seeing what she saw, his fluids almost joined hers, but he turned at the last moment and got out of the bathroom, ending up dry heaving, but nothing else. Confirming it was not actually a hallucination brought by whatever sickness was plaguing her, Andrea moved, and with great disgust, fished out the minuscule hand. Grimy and wet, but with completely intact skin, it was a baby hand severed at the wrist. The soft skin at the joint had tiny holes, like punctures, and the visible meat was light red and glistening, hinting at the white of the bone nestled inside.

"This has to be some weird disease," she said, and her husband took a step away from her at that. Her eyes were burning with tears, but she calmly cleaned the hand with a towel, carefully wiping away the browns and the greens from its skin. It was cold, but not bluish or dark. It was definitely not plastic. She hadn't eaten some weird Halloween toy in her sleep. It was tender, almost alive, a left hand. She expected it to take her thumb and squeeze like it was a part of a real baby in her arms. Something was either terribly wrong, or she would wake up and everything would be actually fine. Or maybe she'd thrown up in her sleep and suffocated on her vomit, and this was some twisted afterlife.

Showing the baby hand and explaining what happened at the ER brought Andrea into the hospital bed where she was thoroughly examined. The rush to the hospital in her Christmas-themed pajamas caused a new bout of nausea, building toward another puking session, along with the rising dread that something terrible could come out next.

The doctors and the nurses flocked around her, like flies feasting on the shit, which was precisely how she felt, exhausted and dirty. A foul smell clung to her skin and breath. Andrea was alone—they didn't let her husband accompany her, and the doctors refused to acknowledge her. Ignoring her pleas for answers, they talked to each other in hushed tones, vibrating with elation. It was her body, her life, and they acted like she was only a textbook problem for them to solve. She thought she knew humiliation, hugging her toilet bowl, and she was promptly shown better.

During the examinations, she threw up the third time. This time it was more difficult, with very little to actually come out, her body shuddering in pain while collecting the last of her meal from the depths of her stomach. With these drops, another big clump traveled, mapping the path usually taken when food went down, now going in reverse. With choking breaths, she pushed out of her the other hand into the metallic washbowl the nurses gave her. The right to fit with the left. At that, the doctors exploded with excitement.

After she'd vomited out a left forearm with threadlike tendrils hanging from one side of it, a group of new doctors showed up, two men and one woman, looking expensive and polished in a way the rest of the hospital didn't. They allowed her husband to join her at her bed, and only then did they finally explain what was going on.

Disassembled baby syndrome, it's what they called it. Her body had created a special gestational bladder in her abdomen, where a fetus developed in parts. The baby was perfectly fine, they assured her, though smaller than usual, explaining something about how the bladder was nutritious and keeping it safe, but that they needed to wait for all the pieces to come out of her and assemble it for it to come alive. *Like a certain chocolate egg toy*, one of the doctors said with a chuckle, the others laughing at his joke.

Hadn't she noticed that she was getting fat, they asked her. She choked on a laugh at that. Of course she had, but there was no indication that her putting on weight was anything other than food. But now she understood why all of that calorie counting and high-protein diets didn't work. In a very wrong sense, she was pregnant.

"I'm sorry," she said at one point, incredulous, "you make it sound like this is a thing that happens."

"It did," one of the doctors said. The one with the joke about confectionery.

"Once before," said the doctor standing to his left. "Somewhere far away. We didn't want to cause a panic, so it wasn't broadcast to the public. But we believe we will see even more of these cases like yours in the future."

"There are theories that this is the new evolutionary stage for humans," said the third doctor, a lone woman out of the three. Andrea hoped to find a compassionate face in her, but the woman was as clinically detached as the rest.

The vomit of medical jargon they projected all over her couldn't hide the fact they were leaving her to throw up foreign body parts piece by piece and then expect her to care for it like a normal child.

"Absolutely no, I want this abomination out," Andrea cut through their noise. She'd wanted to say more but said abomination's right forearm took that opportunity to travel her esophagus, leaving a trail of excruciating pain. For several minutes, the only thing that could be heard was her retching and anguished cries, followed by a loud clunk. Someone took the bowl with the forearm away from her. She saw the same pink tendrils hanging from it as from the left one, soggy and limp.

All of the doctors were solemn, and that never bode well. Through stinging tears, feeling the acidic burn in her scratched throat, unable to move her spent body, she listened to the doctors explaining the situation to her. The recent law prohibited an abortion if there *might* be a heartbeat, something she never thought would concern her because she's always wanted a child. When Andrea pointed out that the baby isn't alive until they assembled it—so why not just open her up and take it?—they reminded her that the law also prohibited a C-section. Only natural births were permitted.

Andrea remembered the news and people freaking out, but she was of the firm belief that natural was always better and that when she became pregnant, she wouldn't even go to the hospital but instead choose home birth. Soon, she'd stopped seeing the social media posts about it anyway, letting that law disappear in the background like anything else that wasn't immediately relevant in her life.

"Don't worry, it's your body doing this, so it's natural," said one of the doctors, again the woman of the three, echoing Andrea's memory. *And natural is always good*, went unsaid. But Andrea didn't believe that anymore. Maybe helping out nature wasn't that bad. She almost started laughing, but there was no strength left in her to even chuckle.

"What happened? You know, last time?" her husband asked. Green in the face, resembling the puke, he was listening to it all wearing a brave face. Andrea wanted him to do more, to rage, to threaten the hospital, the doctors, to take a knife in his hands and open her abdomen himself if need be, to do all the things she desperately wanted to do herself, but couldn't. Her body had crashed out and refused to obey, beyond drained. She could barely lift her fingers.

"Oh, unfortunately, the strain on the body was too much on the mother, and she died," said the first doctor, fixing a sorrowful face that was so fake it could actually be a carnival mask.

"But don't you worry," said the one on his left, looking right at Andrea's husband, "the baby was all right. An alive and healthy boy. After they'd stitched him together, of course."

At no point was Andrea left alone, doctors and nurses always seconds away, ready to jump in at the first hint of a heave, waiting for a new body part. And yet she was never so lonely. Her husband couldn't watch this so he valiantly ran away, but not before he'd tearfully told her how she was the strongest person he knew, and how much he loved her; how everything would be fine, and all three of them would go home to wait for the new year after she puke-birthed their child.

She didn't want to come back to her home with a vomit baby sewn together so that it could be alive. She wanted to die each time a convulsion stretched her insides, lifting a body part to her mouth, crushing her teeth on its way out. Blood coated the pieces, and she begged for some water, or tea, or anything else liquid, hoping it would make things easier to throw up. But they refused, and maybe it was all a moot point anyway because she could feel her body tearing up, destroying with each new shudder, each new push. A table was close to her bed, and on it, glistening body parts rose in numbers. Hands and arms, lower and upper, feet and legs. All disjointed.

She watched the doctors use the rosy tendrils on the extremities to connect the limbs together at the joints, stitching them through the pinprick holes she remembered seeing on the first hand she threw up.

Andrea couldn't speak anymore because her mouth was ruined, her bleeding gums pulsating. She couldn't find a position that would relieve her from agony. They didn't want to give her any pain medication, because the natural was always the best way, and who knew how that would affect the birth. *The birth.* She wanted to weep upon hearing that word but didn't have any tears left in her.

She could only count down the minutes to the next bout of vomiting, of the next body part.

The head came out fine, small and round, with a wrinkled face and cheeks. The eyes of the baby were closed, and it wasn't breathing because it didn't have a chest. That was the last thing that was left waiting in her broken body and she was counting down the minutes toward the blissful end. Alive or dead, at least she would be free of vomiting.

For a brief moment, Andrea wondered if she should try and ask for her husband to say goodbye, but then remembered how he'd left her alone to die, and decided she would rather grasp and hold to that bitter hate she felt for him, hoping it would give her some semblance of strength, or at least comfort in her last moments. To think there was a time she wanted children with that man. She hoped this kid would ruin his life like it was destroying hers.

She thought she already knew pain, that there was nothing that would surprise her. When the torso came, on the wave of a convulsion so strong she thought she'd explode, tearing away the last membranes of her throat, and dislocating the jaw while bursting out in a surge of dark blood, Andrea begged her mind to pass out, only to reach all new heights of suffering. Nurses screamed at her to push, and push, holding her at the shoulders, keeping her upright over the bowl, catching the body forcing its way through the wound of her ripped-open mouth. As soon as they had it, they left Andrea to hit the bed, letting the doctors take over the vomited torso. It had tendrils hanging from the holes at the places where the arms, legs, and head should come.

Andrea was lying drenched in her blood, hollowed out. Through the blurry eyes, she saw the baby coming together in the arms of the doctors. They attached the already sewn-up legs and arms to the body and finished with the head. After the last tendril thread was closed at the neck, the little mouth moved, taking the first breath. The baby's eyes scrunched in, what Andrea thought, was disgust, before it started to shriek.

Is anyone going to stitch me now? Andrea thought. She watched the doctors and nurses examine the baby, completely uninterested in her or the fountain of blood that kept pouring out of her. It was the last thing her consciousness was able to shape before everything turned to black.

DYSTOCIA

Nuno Gonçalves

I suture. Muscle with muscle, skin with skin. The muscle fibers are somewhat frayed, and the edges of the skin struggle to realign. The cut could have been cleaner. Should have, if I had the time.

When I entered the operating room, the baby was already dead. The mother had been anesthetized and laid motionless on the table, but her screams still dripped down the walls. The team members—doctors and nurses—stared at me when I entered, with that expression all sur-

geons fear, those looks filled with hope. In their faces, I could read what they faced, their despair, their swallowed tears.

The silence is such that I can hear the thread crossing through the tissues. If there's one thing to say about the thread, it's that it obeys us. It follows the path we trace with the needle, joining what we want to unite. The thread is our friend because the thread is predictable.

The baby's head hung outside, between the mother's legs. It was a good head, not too large, with thick, dark hair. Back in the day, when I started, babies didn't have so much hair. They've been gaining hair while I lost mine. The baby's body was still inside the womb, stuck by the shoulders, the child's bones wedged against the mother's bones, incapable of leaving or going back to the uterus. I looked at my colleagues, and they returned my gaze, empty of ideas.

Separate stitches, perfectly aligned, symmetrical. Curiously, my hand doesn't tremble, and each knot is precise. A surgeon's hand has no callous, but never look at one's heart.

Sometimes, some days, the only joy that's left is the one we find in technical precision.

The head was already half dislocated, the result of the hopeless use of forceps and possibly fractured clavicles. I asked for the orthopedic kit, and they brought it after a quiet hesitation but without complaints. The sound of the hammer didn't belong to that room, and neither were the instruments used to bones so tender. They did their job, obedient.

I admire the suture. Knots perfectly spaced, with the correct tension, resulting in a strong and compact union. No one will convince me that staples can be a good enough substitute. Using staples is one more sign that humanity is losing the thread, pardon the pun.

I placed the head on the table where the instruments were. No one got closer. Some turned their faces away. I reached the mother, made a slow incision on her abdomen, cut through the tissues, opened the uterus, and freed the decapitated body. It was that of a boy. The resident left the room and we heard him vomit in the scrub sink.

After cleaning up the baby, I cradle him for a moment. I admire the fingers on his hands.

Small, like all the others, but motionless and pale. I wrap him in a white sheet, making an effort to hide the seam around the neck. I put the cap handed by the nurse over the baby's head and tell the anesthesiologist:

"Wake up the mother."

NESTING

Marie Lestrange

"I'M FRIGHTENED OF EGGS, worse than frightened, they revolt me. That white round thing without any holes… have you ever seen anything more revolting than an egg yolk breaking and spilling its yellow liquid? Blood is jolly, red. But egg yolk is yellow, revolting. I've never tasted it."

— *Alfred Hitchcock*

SAVANNAH

As sure as the grass is high, I know it in my heart that this outhouse claiming to be our new home surely wouldn't do. I mean, I know this is New River, but me and my sisters had lemonade stands down in Jackson that were nicer than this sack of a shack we were pullin' up to.

I sigh, rubbing the calloused and rough hand that rests on my swollen belly, fixing my face to make sure my sweet Richard didn't catch sight of my disappointments. We were lucky to have been given this farmhouse. Blessed to call it home.

Even if his grandma did just pass away in it not a fortnight ago.

This wasn't gonna be like those fairytales Momma filled my head with.

Richard rushed around to my side, creaking open the rusty door with a smile that prolly could've fooled our friends at church, but not me. I could see the pain and embarrassment in his eyes. As hard as he'd worked in the mines, I know he wished there was more to show for it. But gamblin' and whiskey had a way of washin' away such things.

Despite it all, I *would* find peace under the weight of the kudzu blanket covering the porch… damn near half the tin roof, if I'm bein' honest.

My threadbare, flowery dress was glued to my skin with sweat. I wiped as much from my bangs as I could, the air more solid than it should be. Thick. Hot. Tempered by the slightest of cool breezes. Thunder rumbled just off in the distance, so faint I could barely hear it. Unthankfully, one of the roosters pecking around in the wildly overgrown front yard crowed to let us know a storm was movin' in quick.

As my husband led me toward the ripped screen hardly covering the paint-chipped front door, my heart sank further. How could we ever make this dilapidated old house into a proper home?

"C'mon now, Vannah," Richard cooed, planting a prickly kiss on my cheek laced with *forgive me*… "You head on inside, and soon we'll get this place all spruced up real nice like I know you're wantin'. Make it feel like home sweet home."

"Sure thing, darlin'," I said, mustering a tired smile despite my doubt. Richard meant well. He worked so hard to provide for our growing family. That accident in the mines just *really* did a number on him.

I thought of the few boxes we brought from our apartment in Jackson, holding the remnants of my old life. Photo albums, my favorite quilt, and the baby clothes Mama and I had sewn every night for the past seven months among them. I could do this. *We* could do this. Like a hen gone to roost, soon enough, I'd turn this place into a warm little nest.

As sure as the rooster crows, I found myself fallin' into a routine that was as steady as the sunrise. Every morning, I'd shuffle out to that rickety coop, my swollen belly leadin' the way, to fetch me an egg. There was something soothing about crackin' that shell, watchin' the yolk sizzle in the pan. It was a small thing, but Lord knows, it felt like the only thing I could control in this topsy-turvy world of ours.

I started spendin' more time with them chickens than I care to admit. Studyin' 'em, like they held some secret I was desperate to uncover. Their cluckin' and peckin' became a sort of language I was itchin' to understand. Meanwhile, inside our little outhouse of a home, I'd fuss over the baby's room somethin' fierce. Arrangin' and reaarangin', like if I got it just right, everything else would fall into place. Before I knew it, there were more rooster figurines than stuffed bears, more hen pillows than baby blankets.

My sweet Richard, bless his heart, he'd call when he could from the mines. But lately, I found myself strugglin' to string two words together without some odd cluckin' sound slippin' out. Not that I noticed, mind you. He'd give me that look through the screen, concern mixed with somethin' else I couldn't quite place.

As the days wore on, I paid less and less mind to my own self. My skin, once soft as a peach, was dryin' up like the creek bed in

August. My frame, already thin as a rail, was wasting away to nothin'. But I couldn't seem to care, not with the whispers that had taken to keepin' me company at night. They'd come floatin' through the baby monitor that didn't even have batteries yet, or maybe it was just in my head. I couldn't rightly say anymore.

That's when things started goin' sideways… real bad. I'd find feathers scattered 'round the house, in places that didn't make a lick of sense. My skin was itchin' somethin' awful, and I'd catch myself scratching till I was raw and bleeding. After one particularly rough call with Richard, I found myself starin' into that old tarnished mirror we'd hung in the hallway. My breath caught in my throat as I could've sworn my nose was changin', hard and growing' longer right before my eyes.

In a moment of clarity, as rare as hen's teeth these days, I tried reachin' out to our old pastor back in Jackson, but shame washed over me like a summer storm, and I hung up before he could even say hello. I was alone out here, truly alone, with nothin' but the kudzu, the chickens, and whatever was happenin' to me for company. Not to mention the little one roosting inside my belly.

Thunder rumbled in the distance, same as it did the day we arrived. But this time, it felt like a warnin'. A storm was brewin', all right, and I had a feeling it wasn't just the weather that was fixin' to break.

As sure as the darkness under a brooding wing, my nights turned into a livin' nightmare. I'd toss and turn, dreamin' of my belly swellin' up like some giant egg, feelin' it pulse and crack beneath my skin. Then it'd burst open, yolk and blood spillin' down my legs like my water breakin'. I'd wake up in a cold sweat, my nightgown clingin' to me like a second skin.

One mornin', I noticed somethin' that near 'bout stopped my heart. Clumps of my mousy blonde hair were scattered on the pillow, replaced by soft, downy feathers. Panicked as a long-tailed cat in a room full of rockin' chairs, I ran to the bathroom, tryin' to pluck them out. My back was raw and covered in goose-

bumps when I was done—but the feathers…
they just kept comin'.

Throughout the day, that stuffed chicken
in the nursery started lookin' awfully real.
I could've sworn I heard soft peeps comin'
from it. Before I knew what I was doin', I was
cradlin' it close, whisperin' soothin' clucks
like it was my own chick. Richard was still
gone… he didn't have to know.

The coop started callin' to me somethin'
fierce. I'd spend hours out there, watchin' the
hens peck and scratch. Found myself mim-
ickin' their movements, my body hunched
over, my steps all jerky-like. When I'd come
back inside, I'd see bugs crawlin' along the
baseboards, and Lord help me, I wanted to
give em' a little taste. Instead, I'd crack open
another egg, watchin' that yolk spill into the
pan, spittin' and sizzlin' like it was tellin' me
all the secrets of the world.

Changin' the baby's diaper became a whole
new kind of horror. One day, I coulda sworn
it was filled with raw egg whites and yolks.
I scrubbed that poor child clean, my hands
shakin' like leaves in a storm. But then…

it wasn't my baby. Not yet. Just the stuffed chicken.

Things were real confusing these days.

Talkin' became harder than pushin' a rope. When our well stopped workin', I tried to call a repairman, but all that came out was clucks and pecks. Frustrated and scared as a rabbit in a wolf den, I retreated further into my own feathered world.

My daily egg ritual became more elaborate than Sunday service. I'd fix 'em every which way–scrambled, poached, fried… and eat 'em like they were manna from heaven. Couldn't stomach nothin' else, convinced that only eggs could keep me goin'.

The stuffed chicken-baby's cries... oh, they changed too. Sounded like tortured squawks to my ears. It drove me to spend more and more time out in that coop, seekin' some kind of peace for my belly and mind.

As I sat there, surrounded by them chickens, I couldn't help but wonder if this was what Grandma felt like before she passed. The thought sent a chill down my spine, colder than a dead witch's tit. Thunder rumbled in the distance, same as always. Another storm was brewin', all right, and I had a clawin' feelin' it wasn't just in the sky.

As sure as cold egg's death, I took to avoidin' mirrors like they was the devil himself. Couldn't bear the thought of what I might see starin' back at me. But wouldn't you know, one day I caught sight of myself in the window, and Lord have mercy, I near fainted dead away.

My skin, once soft as a newborn's bottom, was now a patchwork quilt of feathers and angry red scratches, like I'd been rollin' in a briar patch or plucked rough by a child. My belly had swollen to bursting, a giant egg just waiting to hatch out between my legs. My nose and mouth had gone and hardened into somethin' that looked more like a chicken's beak than any Christian woman's face. And my eyes... well, they wasn't the same innocent browns that used to look back at me. They was wild, and unfocused, like a defenseless hen's when a hungry fox was in the house.

In a rare moment of clarity, I tried to call my sweet Richard. But when I opened my mouth, all that came out was a mess of clucks and squawks that couldn't be controlled, just like the other call. I smashed that phone to kingdom come and flocked again to the chicken coop.

Felt more at home there than I did in that house, if I'm bein' honest.

Now, our new neighbor Mabel, bless her heart, must've gotten worried when she hadn't seen hide nor hair of me in too long a spell. She came 'round to check, and I can only imagine what she found. Our house must've looked like a twister had hit it–feathers and eggshells scattered in a mess, like some unholy confetti of a cock.

And the baby's room... Lord forgive me. All the cute farm decorations we'd picked out, now shredded to bits. In their place, a nest made of blankets and feathers, like some giant bird had taken up residence.

And I knew the bird was me.

I heard Mabel callin' for me, her voice shakin' like a leaf in a storm. All I could do was cluck in response, my voice long gone. As she made her way to the chicken coop, I could picture her face when she saw me—not quite woman, not quite chicken, just peckin' away at the ground like it was the most natural thing in the world.

Poor Mabel, she lit out of there faster than greased lightnin', mutterin' about some curse that had befallen me. "Devil's work," she'd said.

As I watched her go, a part of me wanted to call out, to explain.

But the words wouldn't come. Just more clucks and pecks.

There was that sound again. Maybe thunder? Maybe laughter? The kind that sends chills down your spine and makes you wonder if maybe, just maybe, there are things in this world we ain't meant to understand.

As the clouds gathered, I nestled deeper into my coop, surrounded by my feathered family. Whatever was happenin' to me, whatever curse or demonic mother hen mess had taken hold, I knew one thing for certain—there was no goin' back now. I was in too deep, like the kudzu roots I never did get cleared off the house. The only way out was through.

As sure as secrets rot with time, that final mornin' dawned like any other, but Lord have mercy, it was about to take a turn I never could've seen comin'. I shuffled into the kitchen, my movements more bird than woman now, ready to perform my daily egg ritual one last time. My hands, now talons, shook somethin' fierce as I cracked that egg into the pan.

Instead of the rich, familiar golden yolk I was used to seein', blood came pourin' out like a broken dam. The smell hit me like a freight train, coppery and thick, fillin' the air till I could hardly breathe.

That sight... it was like a switch flipped in my addled brain. Suddenly, I wasn't Savannah no more. I was a mother hen, and by God, I had an egg to lay.

I started cluckin' and peckin' my way through the house, my mind gone to a place I reckon no human mind ought to go. My belly felt like it was on fire, swellin' and pulsin' with each step. I could feel somethin' movin' inside me, pushin' to get out.

When it finally came, there in the kitchen where this whole mess started, it was a sight that would've turned stronger stomachs than mine. Blood and... other things I don't care to name, mixed with feathers on the linoleum floor. The pain was somethin' awful, like bein' split in two, but all I could do was cluck... and purr.

There it was... my beautiful, sweet egg, a porcelain shell for my perfect little chick inside. Without thinkin', I scooped it up in my arms, determined to keep it safe. There was only one place for it now—out in the coop with its true family.

As I stumbled out the back door, the sky opened up and the rain came pourin' down.

I paid it no mind. I had a mission, and come hell or high water, I was gonna see it through.

The chickens scattered as I entered the coop, cluckin' in alarm. I found a corner, nice and warm, and settled in with my precious cargo. As I nestled it close, I couldn't help but wonder if this was how his grandma felt in her final days. Had she the same sense of trouble coming to roost? Nesting in nightmares, I'd started calling it.

The storm raged on outside, but in that coop, surrounded by feathers and the soft peeps of my new family, I felt a strange sort of peace. Whatever I was now, whatever was happenin' to me, at least I wasn't alone no more.

I reckon some stories just ain't meant to have happy endings. But as I drifted off to sleep, my egg tucked safe beneath me, I couldn't help but think that maybe, just maybe, this was where I belonged all along.

Lost in a haze of feathers and confusion, I felt a primal urge swell within me. The kitchen, the coop, the whole entire house… was once a place of warmth and comfort, but now it had turned into a chaotic nest of my own makin'. Today, I was convinced I was nurturing my chick, an instinct that twisted into somethin' dark and all-consuming.

With trembling hands, I lifted the egg I'd laid and carried around with me for days—my little precious. As I poked and prodded at it, the shell began to crack, and instead of the golden yolk I expected, a thick, viscous liquid bled out. The sight sent a jolt through me, blurrin' the line between what was real and what was not.

In flashes of clarity that pierced my site, I caught glimpses of my hands—now claw-like and shakin'—tearin' at somethin' cold and wet. It felt like I was lost in a whirlwind of emotions, battlin' between the instinct to protect and the horror of what I was doin'.

Panicking, I grabbed some duct tape from a nearby drawer and hastily sealed the crack in my egg. It wasn't ready! Not yet. Not yet.

I raced to the kitchen stove, fillin' a pot with boiling water and setting the castiron skillet as hot as it would go. Determined to warm my little precious back to life, I could hear echoes of my baby's cries minglin' with the sounds of sizzlin' eggs in the frying pan. Each crack of an egg felt like a memory slippin' away—scrambled eggs, poached eggs—each one had became a ritual that blurred nurturing with destruction.

Mothering with mayhem.

As I stirred the contents of the pan, I began to hum a lullaby, but it came out as a guttural sound that felt foreign even to me. The kitchen transformed into a nightmarish scene where love twisted into madness. The air thickened with an unsettling mix of blood and egg yolks, swirling together like some terrible reflection of my fractured mind. These eggs would help the baby. They were nice and warm… they'd make it warm, too.

As the sun started settin', castin' long shadows across the room, an overwhelming urge pulled me back to the chicken coop. I could find solace among my feathered friends in there. My transformation felt complete; feathers clung to my skin like the perfect layer, and rusty, dried remnants from earlier chaos marked my body.

Settlin' into a makeshift nest in the coop, surrounded by softly cluckin' hens, I finally found my peace. My chick was safe. Home. Whole.

Savannah the woman faded away like mist in the mornin' as I settled in as a new mother hen.

As night fell over the isolated farmland, my throaty clucks mingled with the sounds of crickets chirpin' outside—a chillin' lullaby echoing through the darkness, wrapped in feathers and shadows as I surrendered fully to my instincts.

I closed my eyes, so heavy, so tired. I heard a car pullin' up the drive. Probably Richard, come home early from the mines. Part of me wanted to call out, to explain, but all that came out was a soft cluck.

·····•·····

WHEN RICHARD RETURNS

Up at 'ta house I heard a sound that made my blood run cold—a cluckin' that weren't quite right comin' from the chicken coop. I nervously made my way over, each step takin' me closer to somethin' I knew in my bones I weren't ready to see.

But nothing could be as awful as all that I'd found in the kitchen.

No. That can't have been real. I was tired from the drive. Hell-u-ci-natin' as I'd heard them brain doctors talk about it.

"Savannah?" I called out. "Darlin', you out here?"

My boots squished and stuck in the mud with sickening slurps and squelches as the muck clung to them. With each step, my boots sank deep, a trail of footprints left behind to carry me on to things I wasn't sure I wanted to know.

She can't have done it. She wouldn't. Had they gotten her, too?

The coop door creaked open… and I froze. Dearest Lord.

God Dammit!

This can't be.

I'd thought she'd be alright here.

Safe among the flock. Safe alone with a baby girl and warm, loving neighbors that *promised* to check in on her every day.

If my heart hadn't stopped working when I saw the remnants of her sanity smeared along our kitchen walls… the floors… the stove… it did now.

For Christ's sake.

I swallowed the vomit tryin' to come up, and stared at the blood-soaked woman before me.

It was my Savannah, but my God in heaven above, it weren't Savannah at all. Great welps of skin speckled her frail body, boils and burns mixed with bubbles of hot glue where she'd feathered her own arms and legs. She was hunched over and squatting, arms tucked in like a foul fucking bird, like she'd forgotten how to stand tall and believed herself to be a chicken.

Our eyes met, and for just a breath, I saw a flicker of my wife in there. But quick as lightnin', it was gone, replaced by somethin' wild and unknowable.

Something demonic, no doubt.

"Sweet Jesus," I whispered, my voice barely there. "What's happened to you?"

Savannah *clucked* at me, her head tiltin' this way and that, like she was tryin' to remember me or figure me out.

My mind raced faster than my boys who tried to get out of that collapsing mine from before, tryin' to make sense of it all. Some things, I reckoned, just ain't meant to be understood.

Why the boys didn't make it out in time.

Why I did.

Why she'd chopped up and fried our baby.

Why I let her.

Whatever had befallen my Savannah, whatever curse or affliction had taken hold of this family, I knew right then and there that there was no living through this.

As I stood there, torn between runnin' and reachin' out to her, Savannah settled back into her nest of feathers and straw, seemin' to forget I was even there. I'd never been so alone in my life as right now.

She was sick. So, so ill. Taken by the devil from the looks of it, but by God, I would try to make her whole. The life we'd dreamed of, the family we'd planned, it had all turned to dust, blowin' away in the wind like so many feathers.

Our mangled babe in the kitchen frying pan, covered in cracked shells and egg yolk, dismembered parts thrown all about the kitchen, wasn't here on earth any more, any-way.

She waited for us in heaven… yes, yes! That's where we'd go.

"Come on, darlin'," I said to my wife. "I'm gonna take us on a little trip away from here." Savannah looked at me, a grin splitting her blood-splattered face. "It's just across the road."

ENGORGED

Rebecca Burgess

I THOUGHT THE WORST part about giving birth would be the actual process of pushing a pumpkin out of my vagina.

I was wrong. God how I wish I wasn't wrong.

All things considered, it went relatively smoothly, besides the overwhelming pain of childbirth. I chose to forego an epidural, though by the time I grew to regret that decision, I was too dilated to change my mind. Sans pain relief, I labored intensely for hours.

Every time the contractions came closer and closer together, the intensity grew as the time between them shrunk and the duration multiplied. The pain was absolutely excruciating, and it felt like my lower back was trying to rip its way out of my skin with each contraction. I've heard back labor is so much worse, and though I've never experienced any other types, I absolutely believe it.

The episiotomy (that the midwife *insisted* was necessary) ripped nearly to my asshole, and I swear I could feel every millimeter that tore my flesh apart. On top of all the torture my body was purposefully going through, I shit myself right on the bed. My husband Corey and midwife tried to hide it from me, but I could tell from the empathetic look in their eyes that I did. The hour of pushing was a completely different level of pain. The burning I could feel in my crotch was like nothing I'd ever felt before. It felt like someone was taking a blowtorch and aiming it directly at my dilated orifice. Johnny Cash's ring of fire had absolutely nothing on this.

As painful as it was, it all ended with me holding the reason behind it all–my sweet, perfect, healthy little baby girl. My absolute world, all in a seven-pound bundle of perfection. I couldn't believe how incredible this little girl was. I couldn't stop staring at her. Even covered in womb gunk, she was the most beautiful thing I'd ever laid my eyes upon. Thankfully the post birth stitching happened while I was in a state of complete euphoria holding this new human I created and grew, so I barely registered that it was even happening. Who knew the best pain relief would be staring into my newborn daughter's eyes?

The midwife and nurse left us for the golden hour: an hour post birth where our little family could bond. Corey and I couldn't stop staring at our little Stella. We wanted to wait to see her in person before we chose a name. We had a few top choices before I went into labor, and we both said her name at the same time. Everything was absolute perfection.

Until it wasn't.

The majority of the hour we spent staring into each other's eyes. She didn't even cry after she was weighed and wrapped up in a swaddle, complete with a cute little hat and bow. With about twenty minutes left, she started rooting. I was dead set on breast-feeding and decided long ago that I would do anything to make it work. Stella latched on perfectly. I thought all was going well until moments went by and she unlatched and kept rooting, getting fussier and fussier as moments passed. I couldn't understand what was wrong and asked Corey to get the nurse even though we still had time left for the three of us. He left the room as our baby's cries became more and more frantic. She was desperate for sustenance.

Moments later, the nurse returned with Corey. She helped me get Stella to latch again, noticing her frantic sucking motions before she pulled away in despair. She noted that no milk dribbled out of her mouth once unlatching, and said that she must not be getting any milk flow. We decided to keep trying and alternating breasts, but it only ended in tears for both of us. I wanted this to work so badly, but I could see the hunger and pleading in my daughter's eyes. That's when I asked the nurse to get me a bottle of formula. She obliged, saying that she would call lactation to come in and see what was going on. I started sobbing, holding my sore chest while Corey rocked our girl, trying to get her to calm down before food would come.

The nurse returned with what I was so far unable to provide for my child. She gave Corey the bottle, and Stella was finally able to eat. She acted like she was chugging it, formula dripping out of the side of her mouth. I cried in pain, emotional and physical, but also in joy that my girl was getting nutrients. Why wasn't I able to give that to her? Why could I grow her inside my body and keep her safe for nine months, but not be able to feed her? My breasts felt completely full, WHY couldn't I get anything to come out? It was almost as if the milk was trapped inside, completely unable to escape its walled off prison cell.

Corey burped Stella for the first time and she finished her bottle, promptly falling asleep as the last few drips flowed out of the nipple. We both stared at her as her chest moved up and down, up and down, up and down, admiring this little creature we created. He asked if I wanted to hold her again. I desperately did, but as I shifted, I noticed the growing pain in my breasts. It wasn't a shooting pain, but more of a throbbing pain, like something was inside and desperate to get out. The milk. MY milk. My milk meant for my daughter.

I opened my gown and looked down, seeing my normally A cup breasts turned into C cups during pregnancy, now even bigger than when I was admitted to the hospital. "Whoooooooaaaaa," Corey said, noticing the growth from even the day before. "Those look painful." No shit, Sherlock. I was about to make the sarcastic remark when I heard a knock. An angel appeared in the doorway.

"Hi there! I'm Emma with lactation. Is it an ok time to come in for an assessment?" I replied with an immediate "YES!" as the relief flowed down my face. She pulled up a chair to the other side of my bed and asked how things had been going. I filled her in on Stella's seemingly perfect latch, how she was unable to get out any milk, and the throbbing pain in my breasts. Emma asked if I'd have any milk let down, and after some thought, I replied that I haven't. My gown had been dry (minus my tears) and I hadn't noticed anything coming out at all.

She said that I might be engorged already, and that's why my milk wasn't flowing. She recommended placing warm washcloths over my breasts before letting Stella latch again, massaging them, and taking a hot shower to see if that would help express the milk. Stella's cries may help move things along too, but that hadn't worked so far. Emma said she'd return in a little over an hour to see Stella attempt to nurse.

Corey placed Stella in the bassinet and grabbed a few washcloths to soak in hot water before wringing them out and bringing them to me. I prayed this would be the relief I needed as I laid them on top of my breasts. It felt soothing, and I was certain this would be it. Nothing felt different, though, and the pain didn't diminish at all besides the initial feeling of the heat. When I removed them to see if any milk had released, they seemed even bigger than before. Thick, blue veins started popping out, mimicking the varicose veins that were now a permanent part of my thighs.

A look of concern flooded Corey's face as he looked in my direction, asking, "Do I… do I need to get the milk lady back in here?"

"Not yet," I responded painfully through gritted teeth, "but can you help me get into the shower?" He carefully helped me out of bed after getting my flip flops and led me to the bathroom. I stopped before entering to glance back at my perfect baby girl. He already had a towel set up for me in there, turned the water on to warm it up, and held my hand as I shuffled into the shower. This was going to hurt like hell, and I had to be careful of my stitches, but I was absolutely desperate to get this milk out.

I felt the steaming water hit my chest. Like before, it felt soothing at first, but the throbbing quickly returned. I started to massage the left breast, starting with the outside of my breast and moving towards the nipple, just like the lactation consultant said to. Nothing except clear water traveled down.

We could hear Stella start crying, and Corey left the bathroom to collect our girl. I looked down, hoping that I would see that yellow tinge of colostrum drip out of my breasts, but still only saw water. Not even a slightly opaque white color emerged. The pain intensified, and I could swear I saw my breasts grow in size before my eyes. They weren't this big before I got in the shower, were they?

I called for Corey to come back in, hoping that he could tell me otherwise, but before he could enter the bathroom, they grew again, a small but noticeable amount, now about the size of cantaloupes. *How can this be happening?* I wondered in a panic, hoping that Corey would barge through the door and tell me I was hallucinating. My chest felt heavier as I waited, so I sat on the shower chair as the hot water poured all over my seemingly growing breasts. I got extremely tired, my vision blurred as I laid my head against the wall. The last thing I remembered was hearing Corey yell for a nurse before my world turned to black.

....

I woke up lying in my bed, soaking wet and groggy, chest throbbing worse than before, with several unfamiliar nurses surrounding me. Corey stood in the background, holding our sleeping Stella, fear written all over his face. "... Babe?" I barely called for him as my brain thought about what happened before this.

He tried to come forward, but a nurse stopped him. "Dad, we just need you and baby girl to keep back for now. I promise you can see Mom after we evaluate her." He took a step back, clearly shaken by my appearance.

I barely had to look down before I gasped. My breasts had nearly doubled in size since the shower. "What... What's happening to me?" I whispered to myself, hoping a nurse would overhear. I peered around the room at the numerous faces, the lactation consultant being the only familiar one. I could tell that even she was trying to hide her confusion. She was on the phone with what I could assume was her superior, trying to get them to come down and see the insanity for themselves. She ran out of the room along with a nurse.

I finally found my voice and asked, "Why are they so big? Why do they hurt so much?"

A nurse, poker face initiated, said "Well, we're trying to get your milk to come out, but it's being feisty and doesn't want to."

I was confused. I'd done plenty of research on breastfeeding while I was pregnant, I had never read anything about them filling up with milk and engorging to this extent. "Have you ever seen anything like this?" I whispered through the throbbing pain.

"We've seen a lot of things, honey," said the nurse. *Nice deflection there*, I thought.

While one nurse was checking my vitals, Corey pulled a different one aside, whispering but still loud enough for me to hear. "Have they grown in just the last minute?"

I looked down. They clearly had.

Emma, the nurse, and two doctors came running in with hot towels and a massage tool to attempt to get the milk to let down. She gasped as she looked at me, rushing over to place the towels down on my chest. This time, the soothing feeling never arrived–just more throbbing, intensifying pain. I could feel them growing by the second. How was this possible??

I closed my eyes from the pain, all the voices in the room jumbling together into one.

"Her temp is 103.5."

"We need to start antibiotics for possible mastitis and cabergoline to suppress milk production."

"We still have to give her something for pain, no way will Tylenol cut it here."

"Have you seen anything like this before?"

"They're bigger than they were a minute ago."

"Dad, we're going to need you and baby to head to the nursery for a little bit."

"What? Is she going to be alright? Please tell me you know how to help her. PLEASE."

Don't leave. Corey, I need you. Stella. Come back. I just want to hold my baby girl. Please let me hold my baby... I thought, but couldn't speak through the pain. Then the pressure started. The pain intensified. The sobs that I had already been emitting turned into screams. I opened my eyes again to see two beach balls covered in a thinning layer of skin directly on top of my chest. "WHAT IS HAPPENING TO ME?" I shrieked as the nurses and doctors discussed prepping the OR. Operating room? Why the operating room?

I never got to find out what they were planning.

I felt a tearing sensation and heard a ripping sound. The towels covering my chest began turning a deep shade of red. The nurses removed them, and I could see the skin on my breasts began slowly splitting apart, blood dripping from the fresh, growing wounds. Someone took the brakes of my bed off as the others started clearing the way. "We need to get her there NOW."

The bed started to move as the blood turned into a waterfall, gushing out of the now gaping crevasses in my still growing breasts. The bed passed by the nursery, where I saw the loves of my life staring at me through the window, Corey openly sobbing as he ran to it. Just as he did, the dam burst. My breasts burst open like Gallagher watermelons, a milky, bloody combination of liquid and gore covering everything and everyone in sight. Even through the glass, I could hear Corey's screams and Stella's cries fill the hallway as I lost consciousness.

TAKE THE BABY

Peter J. Larrivee

"Take the baby."

Three words I have come to hear in my nightmares and waking dreams. I love my son dearly. He is my whole world. Maybe it's an evolution thing, maybe I'm just the sentimental type, but since the first time I looked into his dark eyes, I knew he would be the only thing I could ever focus on again.

I was right there the whole time while my wife, Britta, pushed and cried with joyful agony. The midwife announced it was a boy, and I welled up with pride. He did not come out crying, but oddly calm, serene even. I saw the head crown, and I watched as the blood and viscera of the afterbirth slid out, following the baby. It didn't bother me. Some people have trouble with all of that, but this was the most important moment of my life, and I went into it with a sense of wonder and awe.

They put him on Britta's chest, and the newly named Alan began to move his heavy head, struggling with muscles that had never moved such weight before. His head turned, his eyes opened, and locked on mine.

I'm told babies can't see more than a few inches in front of them at birth, but from ten feet away, while I was grabbing water for my wife, I looked back, and eyes as black as ash looked into mine. I felt something within me change forever, like my entire life had new purpose. I was no longer my own man, I was father to a tiny creature that needed me. I couldn't imagine any other way to live.

That was three months ago. Britta's tail-bone had cracked during the birth, she tore in three places, and because of how fast the birth was (thirty minutes of pushing, two hours of labor), there was some minor internal damage as well. We stayed in the hospital for three days. She had some minor surgery, and she was told to stay in bed until she healed, which would take months.

This worked fine, since she intended to co-sleep and breastfeed twenty-four seven. We'd seen some documentary about formula, and she was now vehemently against the stuff. She could be very stubborn. She wanted Alan's entire food supply to come from her.

So for the next three months, she stayed in bed, and I slept on the couch for fear of rolling over on the little guy. I went back to work, but I couldn't go full-time. Every few hours the call would come in, and I'd have to rush home to take the baby. She needed to pee, or eat, or sleep, or bathe, and I'd spend hours calming him and bouncing him, singing and rocking, making faces and exhausting myself to get him to settle. Sometimes I could even get him to sleep, but never for very long, not without my wife's breasts there for him to nurse from. That was what he knew, and that was what he wanted.

The house went to shit. Dirty dishes piled up. Food was scarce as I could never get away long enough to go shopping, and little dust bunnies began multiplying. My efforts to clean or cook or even just breathe and take stock of things was always broken by that piercing cry, and the words: "Take the baby."

By month two, she'd lost the baby weight. I'd taken to bringing home mountains of cheap fast food just because it was all I had time for. I didn't sleep well, either, as my self-imposed isolation on the couch only assured me quiet time in the dark, but not comfort. The couch was too plushy, and my neck always felt at an odd angle.

I'd sleep two hours at a time, maybe, and then I'd hear *that cry*. That shrill cry that would jerk me awake and fry my brain, send my pulse racing and cortisol spiking. Adrenaline would make me leap from the couch and run upstairs into the room where my son would be wailing, my wife, wide awake with exhausted eyes and a pale complexion would say: "Take the baby."

Then, a quick three steps to the changing table, wet diaper off, wipe down, powder, clean diaper on—I'd gotten it down to a precision drill. Before the plume of airborne talc could settle, I had the baby changed, re-dressed, and ready to go back to the breast. But he wouldn't go back right away, oh no, that would be too easy. I first had to hold him and bounce him, singing a nonsense song that became my only coherent thought.

"Go to sleep, baby boy, a bouncing baby boy—
Go to sleep, little boy, a bouncing baby boy"

The lyrics didn't matter. What mattered was the hour it took to calm him down and get him back to the breast. I could have been singing Black Sabbath to that tune. As long as I sang, he remained quiet—blissfully, mercifully quiet. If I stopped, that banshee wail would resume.

Then, if I was lucky, I'd get two more hours of sleep. Then another cry. More panic. And just when I was too frustrated to think straight, he'd look at me with that smile, that perfect, wide, adorable smile, with wide dark eyes that always looked right into my soul, and I'd be his slave once again.

By the end of month two, I was so sleep deprived that I was hallucinating at my desk. I'd take phone calls without picking up the phone, I'd fall asleep on conference calls and once I had a dream that the phone rang for me, my wife repeating my new mantra over and over as I stared blankly at a monitor screen: *"Take the baby. Take the baby. Take the baby."*

Coffee and grim determination kept me going, but I had to take a lot of days off just to take care of wife and baby, or maybe even grab some vital, nourishing naps during the day. My long absence was intolerable to little Alan, and I could barely get my foot in the door at night before I'd hear the words: "Take the baby."

I didn't understand how other people could do this. Babies weren't supposed to fuss this much, were they? I called the pediatrician, who told us to bring him in. A quick visit and a fifty-dollar co-pay later, and she was stumped. I called the midwife, who told me everything would be okay as long as he kept going to the breast. He was a little young to be teething, but that might be a slim possibility. She asked how my wife was doing, and I told her she'd been losing a lot of weight.

"Lots of fatty food," she said. "She needs nutritious fat from good sources. Stuff her. She's feeding the little one who needs every calorie he can get. Do that, and everything should be fine."

So I soldiered on, waking in the night thinking the blinking lights on the smoke detector were red eyes watching me, or that the shadows would make some slithering skittering noise. Those were the bad nights, when I found myself so disconnected from my senses that a light wind could make me feel as if something were breathing on my neck from behind.

Then the cry. Then the words. "Take the baby."

But I get it now. I understand, because last night, it all started to make sense in a beautiful kind of grotesqueness. I found myself lying and staring at the swirling multicolored dots that speckled the pitch black, the error messages of the brain trying to find a pattern in the gloom. I thought I could see grinning faces of strange things that would then slither away into the black. I was sure I was half-dreaming as the winged thing with red eyes glided soundlessly past and towards what I think was the stairway, and with a whoosh of flapping wings, shot upwards towards the landing.

A creak in the dark from somewhere upstairs shook me fully awake. I knew that creak. It was the bedroom door. I heard it in my dreams and nightmares, always immediately before the words, "Take the baby."

Then I heard the cry, that horrible shrill cry, jarring me from any possible thought and sending me bolting faithfully up the stairs. I knew my way through the dark, past all the hallucinations and half-dreams to the bedroom, where there was a pale red light. Was it red? Or were my eyes still half-closed? I willed them to open fully, but the red did not disappear. Something bathed the room in an unnatural red glow, like a dying fire.

There in the bed, the blankets pulled down, was Britta. Her skin was porcelain white, but mottled by black spots all over her hairy, un-shaven, atrophied legs. Dark stains surround-ed her on the mattress and walls as her chest was open, bare, bleeding and dripping loose fat from the mauled breasts. She turned to me with a wide, manic smile. Her emaciat-ed form raised its toothpick arms, struggling to hold up the nine-pound screaming thing that was my son. The red glow burned like dying embers behind his dark eyes, and the spreading wings from his back began to beat against my weakened wife's arms. Fingernails like black claws tore into her papery skin, shedding dark blood. I heard her weak, raspy voice: "Take the baby." At my approach, the tiny, winged thing with dark eyes smiled at me.

Then I was his slave.

THE ANIMUS OF AGNES GRISHOM

Deborah Coldiron

(Excerpt from *A Brief History of Saint Agnes Township* by Phineas Pembroke, 1846)

In the year 1793, Oakland Township was rechristened Saint Agnes Township after our patron saint Agnes Grishom. Although she will never be recognized by the Vatican, she will be forever venerated by the local townsfolk for her brave accomplishment. I share this story here just as it was told to me by my grandmother, Emma Pembroke, a direct descendant of Agnes and Donagh Grishom through their 4th son Ezra.

There exists not one thing on God's good Earth more terrible than the birth of a child. Wondrous, too; but ask any woman whose hour of travail approaches, and she will speak of the terror it inspires.

Yet the joy that follows brings with it a most powerful amnesia. And so, women return to the marriage bed. Agnes Grishom had faced the dreadful circumstance of parturition six times already. Six times Agnes had emerged triumphant. And for her efforts, six sons. Healthy and robust, the very foundation of Agnes's home often quaked at the roiling excitations of her brood, and she delighted in them as much as any mother could.

But autumn had been dark and dismal, and it left Agnes weary. The inevitable approach of her seventh labor filled the woman with a kind of dread that was at once strange and familiar. Familiar, in that the act of childbirth is wrenching and miserable work, fraught with dangers both known and unknown—dangers Agnes had faced and endured many times before. Strange in that *this* time, she knew there was a threat of an entirely new kind.

A presence within her swelled and grew so strong that Agnes could scarcely hear her own thoughts. But it was not the spirit of an innocent child that vexed her. By some terrible knowing, she realized *two* occupied one space in her womb. Just as Jacob and Esau wrestled within Rebekah's belly, there was a tumultuous battle between light and dark within Agnes as well.

Donagh good-naturedly teased her, dismissing her fears as nothing more than the dreadful fancies of an anxious mother, but Agnes was resolute in her understanding. She was neither hysterical nor prone to delusion. There was, indeed, another within her—one whose nature was *preternatural*, whose origins seemed drawn from the foulest recesses of the abyss. This was no nightmare conjured by an excitable mind.

The presence she felt inside her was so foreign, so corrupt, it could not be human. Agnes had a foreboding that this creature was some sort of malefic aberration, but also, she could feel that it was unmistakably *female.* Like Lilith in the days of Eden, though made from earth, this demon daughter would not be earthbound. In her sleep, Agnes saw vivid images of a winged witch, a harpy, sent to them by the Devil himself. She wondered if the creature's face would resemble her own face? Would its body be like hers, or that of a vulture? Would it fly from the birthing table on awful black wings? And what might this abomination do to her innocent bairn?

A few months prior, an encounter in the village had deepened her unease. Walking home with her husband and sons after Sunday service, Agnes fell behind. She had trouble matching Donagh's prodigious strides, slight as she was, and that day he was in a particular hurry. Her sons ran behind their father, burning off the bountiful energy stored during long morning prayers. It was the anniversary of their youngest son's christening, and the boys all knew their favorite meal was waiting for them at the house—venison pie with leeks and sweet onions, asparagus soup, and at the young boy's request, cranberry and spiced apple cornbread.

Not wanting to make them wait, she picked up her pace as she walked, now alone, past the old country graveyard. The place had always disturbed Agnes—it was dark, no matter the time of the day. Overgrown oriental bittersweet had long ago obscured the view through the cemetery fence, inside the invasive vines had smothered all woody plants, having climbed and weighed down the delicate hemlock branches long ago. Agnes could see mottled shadows stirring behind the gate and it made her shiver.

Relief dawned as she reached the end of the wrought iron barrier, but as she rounded the corner, she collided with a towering man. To be precise, she collided with the *basket* the man was carrying. Root vegetables tumbled to the ground and scattered, rolling in all directions. Agnes immediately dropped to her knees, scrambling to gather the beets, turnips and russets. She was startled by how quickly her mood shifted from apprehension to embarrassment. Her cheeks filled with sudden heat, and then Agnes felt the chill of a dark shadow engulf her. The man was kneeling as well, his lanky frame blocking the late morning sun. He was not gathering the spilled roots. She stole a glance at his face. Agnes did not know this man. He was perhaps ten years her senior, with a strong angular jaw and a carefully arranged mop of coal black hair. She saw instantly that he was handsome, but imposing. She chastised herself for letting Donagh get so far ahead of her, as she hurried to complete the task at hand.

The man spoke, his smooth voice was penetrating. Agnes stopped breathing. "I will tell you a secret, if you promise to keep it… Agnes," her name left his lips in a long hiss. *How did this man know her Christian name?* Wary of the stranger, Agnes clamored to her feet and tried to put some distance between them, but the man's long fingers clutched her arm, pulling her back with considerable strength. His free hand found her belly and something in her womb stirred with recognition at his touch. *That was impossible. It was too soon to feel a baby move at this stage.*

"You carry two, and two shall be," the man crooned. "One for you, and one for me."

The pungent odor of sumac and chicory wafted from his coat as he leaned close to Agnes's face. She looked up and their eyes met—in that instant Agnes's blood ran cold. His eyes were not the eyes of a man; they glinted with an unnatural, hellish light. Seeing the realization wash over her, his mouth stretched into a wide, supercilious grin. Agnes knew at once she was looking into the face of the Devil. Gasping for air, she tore herself free and fled, her heart pounding. Though the distance between them grew with every frantic step, the sting where his fingers had gripped the flesh below her navel remained. Tears of pure terror escaped and ran down her cheeks. Wicked laughter erupted behind her, but when she finally dared to look back, she saw that he had disappeared.

The memory haunted Agnes. Dread seeped into their home at night, under the doors and through the cracks in the windows. The chill of it reached the bones in her feet and crawled up her legs in frigid veins until it reached her heart. She would have thrown herself from a cliff to end this evil, were it not for the sacred duty she bore to her town, her family, her unborn child, and if male—a seventh son! Agnes suspected her brush with Hell that holy day confirmed she carried a blessed boy, but also the Devil's child—a daughter of the damned.

If God willed it and the Grishoms produced another male heir—one born seventh in an unbroken line of sons, just as his father had been—then the babe would be the Seventh Son of a Seventh Son. Such a boy would be an asset to their whole community—a healer, a seer—just the charm they all needed to be cured of the Great Sin. The village would need him to survive the bitter winter ahead, plagued as they had been with drought and disease these past several years.

Some thirty winters past, the village endured a season of extraordinary severity, one that tested the resolve of its people. It was a season of such bitter cold and despair that even the sun seemed unwilling to shine. The fields lay barren under frost, the rivers froze nearly solid, and an unnatural blight fell upon them. Governor Whitaker, a man of unshakable faith and steady resolve, held the town together through a good many bleak, desolate days. Yet the grim specter of death arose, casting a long shadow over them, ushering in what came to be known as the Starving Time.

It began when a strange dark mold crept into their food stores, the fine mycelium strands burrowing deep within the dry goods, defying all efforts to remove it. Next, it affected the canned fruits and vegetables, as if the fungus had been present since before the time of harvest. Meat could no longer be preserved; it turned to rot so quickly, they struggled to make use of it. Whitaker had rallied the people to salvage what they could. Yet it was no use. Nourishment became scarce. As their bodies grew gaunt, fear and doubt took hold. By midwinter, the oldest among them began to fall like withered leaves.

The governor buried his father on the first of January; by nightfall, he had dug a second and third grave for his two youngest sons. His once-steady hand trembled on the spade, his tears freezing before they could fall to earth. So many followed, that one could scarcely name all of them. By the time the governor's own wife perished, a panic had set in. Whitaker himself lost his way. Inside a fever dream of grief, he made a calamitous decision.

They would have to eat their dead.

The townsfolk protested at first, crossing themselves and wailing, but they had lost so much—573 of their own gone to the grave. It was just too much to bear, and hunger gnawed sharper than conscience. Whitaker led by example, slicing the first unholy portion from the lifeless body of his wife. His eyes burned with shame as he fed the morsel to his only daughter, her lips blue and thin.

The gruesome practice saved 164 lives that winter, but it came at the expense of their souls. The townsfolk, once bound by faith and community, now avoided one another, burdened by shame—believing the Sin so great, even the Lord Jesus would not forgive it. They walked the streets with downcast eyes, unable to meet their neighbors' gaze, and it was said that the land itself had absorbed the Great Sin, leaving a darkness that would not lift.

This was the shadow into which Agnes Grishom was born, and it was this stain she prayed her unborn child would cleanse. The townsfolk believed that only the Seventh Son of a Seventh Son could redeem them of the barbarous transgression and restore their souls. With his power to heal, he could reconsecrate the land and lead them into the future. They all watched expectantly as Agnes's stomach swelled, hope apparent in every stare. She averted her gaze, her eyes darting quickly downward. She hoped too, but not just for a healthy son. She hoped the foul creature within would not tear the child limb from limb before birth.

As the frigid fall waned, Agnes's abdomen grew impossibly large, as though her womb struggled to contain a tempest within. Her round face thinned and her warm complexion grew ashen. The midwives whispered amongst themselves, their hands hesitant as they examined her roiling belly. "It is an ill omen," the older woman had murmured when she thought Agnes could not hear. "No woman carries so, only those who birth monsters." The women fretted and fussed, but they did not gossip, and they did what they could to keep Agnes in good health.

On the night of her confinement, the wind howled fiercely about the house, rattling shutters and tearing at the thatch as though some malign force sought entry. The room was dimly lit by flickering candlelight. Agnes writhed in agony, her cries mingling with the storm's fury.

Her husband and sons waited impatiently in the village, as was custom, while the two midwives attended to Agnes. The women were sisters and both superstitious by nature. One nervously fiddled with the kettle, the other squeezed Agnes's hand, a nervous expression on her face.

Between courses of pain, one thought scared Agnes the most. It would not be enough for her son to survive the birth, although that itself would be a miracle. She felt the two wrestling inside her, angular limbs violently moved under her skin in tempestuous, jarring waves. She imagined a pair of thin, bony talons clawing and scraping at the defenseless infant.

The townsfolk had linked their salvation to this child, but the chilling reality was this: if the she-devil were delivered first, her son would not be a Seventh Son at all.

Oh God, how the Devil must have reveled in the cruel work of chance he had devised!

When her waters broke, the briefest moment of relief washed over her, but it was swiftly replaced by a terrible pressure, labor overtaking her before Agnes could even draw breath. The awful hour had arrived. Agnes cried out to the Almighty to save them.

But her prayers went unanswered, for what emerged first from between her thighs was onyx black, wet and resembled the articulated wing of a bat. The repulsive limb shot out further toward the elder midwife, unfurling to reveal an intricate network of elongated digits stretched taut with translucent membranes of veiny flesh. The woman shrieked, her wrinkled hand instinctively covering her mouth as she beheld the unnatural limb. Her sister, eyes wide with horror, grasped the older woman's arm. With cries that pierced the storm's howl, they fled, leaving the door open to the raging storm and Agnes bare and vulnerable on the birthing table.

Agnes knew all would soon be lost. Her thoughts turned to her six boys, her husband, and the cherished home they had built. She thought of her town and of all the people who had placed their hope in this night's outcome. The pain of labor poisoned her mind, but with great effort, she wrenched it back into focus. At once, she recalled how Esther saved God's people from destruction. Like Esther, Agnes held the fate of the people in her hands. Esther's words from chapter four, verse sixteen rang in her mind, "If I perish, I perish."

Agnes reached for the midwife's blade and in one fierce motion, she cut herself from pubis to navel. Her own blood flooded over trembling hands, making them slick. Sliding through her fingers, the heavy knife clanged loudly against the stone floor as Agnes steeled herself for one final effort. A contraction hit her like a stone and she felt the creature being pushed from her body. There was so little time left.

With preternatural resolve, Agnes plunged her blood-soaked hands into her own pelvic cavity, struggling to gain purchase of the slippery amniotic sac. Failing at that, she began desperately to tear at the caul with her fingers. At last, she broke through the membrane and felt for the child's head. With one smooth tug, she lifted the boy out of her womb and slid him up to her chest. The blade out of reach, she took the cord between her teeth, bit down hard and pulled, ripping the tough flesh to separate them. She tucked the boy safely against her shoulder and melted with relief when she heard his first cry. After a brief awareness of her accomplishment, Agnes Grishom took her final breath and died. After a time, so did the demon trapped between her legs.

When dawn broke, the storm had passed and the house stood eerily quiet. The day's first light glistened off a crimson pool on the stone floor, and the infant's chest rose and fell in equal intervals. In the town, Donagh Grishom and his six young sons began the long trek home in muddy boots. As they emerged from the wood and entered the clearing, his little house appeared. His heart sank abruptly. The front door stood open wide, a silent scream escaping its gaping mouth. He broke into a run.

As his shadow darkened the threshold, the man was struck still. Painfully he struggled to interpret the hideous scene: his wife splayed open, her abdomen rent and gory, a vampiric wing hanging limp from her sex. He fell to his knees.

A phantasmal sound broke the silence, an ethereal cry from somewhere in the house. Donagh raised his head and scrutinized the room. It came from the birthing table. He approached his wife's corpse with apprehension, erupting with grief. There he discovered his newborn son, stirring from a fitful sleep in his cold wife's arms. Understanding washed over him, and his gaze shifted to find his wife's face. *How could she have known what was to come?* His heart broke for Agnes, the evidence of her abysmal suffering laid bare before him, evidence too of her victory over an abomination.

Scooping up the precious child, he swiftly covered his wife with a bed linen, and dashed from the house lest the boys see their mother in such a traumatic state.

Although the night had claimed Agnes Grishom, the dawn bore witness to her triumph. In her final act, she bridged the chasm between darkness and hope. The storm that raged within and without had passed, and with it, the shadows that plagued the township began their long retreat. Her innocent blood consecrated the soil, her sacrifice hallowed the child. In her death, she delivered life—and with it, the promise of redemption.

—The solemn words of Mrs. Emma J. Pembroke on the Seventh of July, 1846.

THERE WAS A NUMBER SEVEN

Patricia Lameida

THERE WAS A NUMBER one.

When Mom found out, she made me drink the tea, so thick it was almost soup, so bitter it burned my stomach. She made me a doll out of one of Dad's socks (a plain black sock like the ones he wore whenever he went to work), and told me to put up with it, that this was what being a woman was all about.

Then I bled, and bled, and bled, and Mom didn't wash the sheets. She told me that if I slept in them, it wouldn't happen again, and she was right.

I don't know if it was the smell or the image, but the truth is that Dad never came back to my room.

There was a number two.

Pimple George was often alone and cried. He had dry hair and long arms and when he cried it was as if he was calling for me. I always listened more than I spoke, and I let Pimple George cry while I listened. He liked to move his arms while he cried, and he was strong when he showed sadness, and he hit hard to exorcise anger.

When Mom found out, she didn't ask. This time I drank more of the tea, a lot more. It was so thick that it was like soup, a soup so bitter that it burned my stomach. Then I bled and bled and washed the sheets myself.

I stole a sock from the gym when Pimple was at training (a white, ribbed, knee-high sock with a pair of rackets on it). And Mom taught me how to make a doll out of it. She told me it was important to learn.

There was a number three.

Number three was Miguel's distraction. When he brought me to this house, he liked to sleep in my bed. We didn't always sleep, we often trained. We trained and slept, and we weren't always alone, and the training wasn't always easy, but he was a hard-working teacher. He liked to teach us in person.

When I told him, he hit me. He kicked me in the stomach a lot while explaining that we had to get rid of it, that there was no place to raise it in this house.

I didn't need any tea, nor did I call Mom. I bled shortly after Miguel left me, lying on the bedroom floor, and the floorboards were so soaked that I still haven't managed to get the stain out. I try every time I mop the floor.

I kept one of Miguel's socks when he first laid in my bed (it was a colorful sock, full of skulls superimposed in fluorescent colors, which still glow whenever I open the drawer). Mom said that women understand these things and, as in so much of what she told me, Mom was right. I made the doll out of that sock and it's the biggest doll in my drawer.

There was a number four.

By the time I realized it had arrived, it was already tapping to the rhythm it felt from the men who visited me. The ones who paid Miguel what he asked for. I didn't have to tell, because it became obvious. And it was with the complaint that I was becoming sluggish and lacking in energy that Miguel found out. He tried kicking me, but even though I was bleeding it wouldn't leave.

So, Miguel called one of the older women. She was the one who shuts up but knows. She told me to lie down and open up, as she found a long needle among the old towels she spread out under me. It was a brown blunt needle, and the woman told me how many socks she had knitted with it. She told me about the colors and shapes, as the needle entered me. She talked about the stitches and the patterns, as she turned the needle on it, on number four, which I felt clawing inside me.

Blood dripped to the rhythm of the words the woman let out. Usually silent, the woman knitting the loss of number four pulled out words to keep me company. And then it stopped struggling. The explanation of yarn and stitches became rhythm as fragments of blood flowed down the thick cloths.

When she finished, the woman cleaned me up and helped me to my feet, tucked a rag of towel between my thighs and let me take her to the drawer where my three dolls were.

The next day, the older woman returned. Her features were heavier because she had seen more, and her mouth was quiet because she had used all the words she had to give me. She sniffed the soaked cloth between my thighs, changed it for a cleaner, less rough cloth, tucked my thighs in and pulled out a knitted sock doll from under her blouse (it was a thick, softly colored sock, made into a round doll). She opened my drawer and carefully laid it down next to the brothers.

There was a number five.

I learned to count my days and steal the socks of the men who visited me when I realized I was late. One day I knew for sure which sock I should keep (a brown sock, torn at the heel, with threads pulled out by so much use).

I hid the sock just as I hid it from everyone. I tried to stay energetic, to please the visitors as Miguel had trained me to do. When I felt it kicking, like someone in a hurry to open a door, I became more vigilant.

Whenever Miguel or one of the men arrived, I covered my belly with the sheet. It was very effective to expose the breasts or the sex and let them come without preamble. And it worked, I kept it with me until it got too big. Then, Miguel stopped pretending he didn't know, and decided it was time to end it.

He didn't call the older woman. He took me from this house to a shack that I couldn't tell where it was. In the shack lived a man, as wide as he was bent, and it was with him that I spent that week, with the man who never spoke.

For the first three days he made me take lots of pills. White and pink, some bigger, some smaller, but always in odd numbers and always with a meal. And the meal was always soup. So thick and so bitter that it burned me from the inside. After three days, number five stopped moving. And the man never spoke.

Then came the pain. And the liquid and the blood and a body that my insides spat out with relief. The man watched, cleaned it all up and never spoke. In a few hours Miguel came back, and, with him, I returned to this house.

Number five was the only one I waited for. I kept the doll wrapped in a piece of pink cloth, just as I would have wrapped it if it could have been spoiled.

There was a number six.

I found out the day it was conceived. I hid the sock (blue, with a yellow heel and wavy scratches on the shin) and prepared the tea, the same one Mom gave me, and let it burn me from the inside and let the blood flow.

And it didn't happen again, until...

This is number seven.

The counterfeit whisky, which I have been using for douching my insides, didn't avoid it, but I don't want it.

I have the sock saved since it arrived (grimy from sweat, thinner at the heel from use) and I've tried everything I can to get rid of it: the soup-thick tea that scalded me from the inside; the blunt needle that made me bleed and limp for a month; the counterfeit pills that left me nauseous and cramping for weeks. And it didn't leave.

It didn't leave and quickly took up space. This time Miguel wanted it to stay, because he found out that some of the visitors paid extra for a pregnant woman. And I've had many, many visitors over the last few months. When I became too big to roll over easily on the mattress, they stopped looking for me.

It was too late for any of the frequent solutions, and I'm too used up to merit any major investment. So, my room is closed, and I'm locked in.

I started to feel pain a few hours ago. I moan softly and know I'm alone from the nothing I hear outside these walls. Miguel emptied the house for this moment, suddenly assailed by some kind of foreboding.

While the pain runs through me in waves, I walk around the room supported by the walls. Little by little, it tears me as it finds its way through my insides. I'm not frightened by the red thread that runs thickly down my legs, I've seen it so many times. But when my knees give way and I realize I can't keep walking, I feel alone.

I drag myself to the drawer. Arranged in a row, snuggled together, my six dolls offer what no one else has stayed to give. Slowly, I take advantage of the interval between pulls and take them out one by one. I let myself slip and hold them, all six of them, in my arms. The urge to push is impossible to control, and so number seven comes out of me, with a weak moan that accompanies my crying, snot and absence.

The blood pours out in gulps. My six little ones are impatient and soon slip out of my arms to join their brother. I look at them: all seven together on a crimson blanket, and smile at the beautiful family I've created. All my children are with me.

So I can close my eyes.

DON'T SAY A WORD

Autumn Weese

I DIDN'T PLAN TO be a mother. It wasn't a forgone conclusion for me the way it was for others. Still, some bits of knowledge are like rites of passage.

Never look a gift horse in the mouth.

When opportunity knocks, open the door.

Never wake a sleeping baby.

And other pieces of advice you gather without suspecting they will ever apply to you until—suddenly—they do.

A public restroom is an inauspicious place to be born. Especially the lonely, single stall in the dog park I walk through on my way home, abandoned by dogs and humans alike to the late hour.

This is a keepsake book—another one of those ideas passed down with a warning that you'll forget the moments that seem most important—so rest assured.

This story wouldn't be here if it didn't have a happy ending. Would it?

Years ago, there was a show called *I Didn't Know I Was Pregnant*. It was a reality show I'd watch on nights I couldn't sleep, and it will be a distant memory by the time you can read this. The title gives away the entire premise and begs the question: how can anyone not know? How can anyone spend most of a year creating a separate life within them without ever suspecting?

I ask you this in return: how *else* does someone end up giving birth in a public restroom?

Anyone can tell you about the pain. Even a sterile book about anatomy can give you nightmares. "Dilation" sounds simple but is the product of hours of impossible pain. Muscle and skin tear as they expand, and only a fraction will ever heal.

It's a wonder anyone survives it.

It's a wonder anyone chooses to do it at all.

I knew about the pain, but no one had prepared me for the absolute terror of uncertainty. The helpless feeling of being caught up in a process that is entirely out of your control and yet totally dependent upon you. The conflict of feeling responsible for every movement while everything important in the world is in someone else's hands.

Everything in my hands. My hands, sticky from the film left behind on the tiled floor. Earlier in the day—several days ago?—some city employee had left it to dry after a hasty mop. There was no way for them to know this would serve as a delivery room.

I wondered how I'd ever really get you clean after. If it was possible.

"Help. Can you help me?"

The words were a nearly exhausted litany whispered against the grimy, tiled floor.

I slowed my breath. In and out. A painfully demonstrative act, all for show.

I'd seen enough movies to know what it should sound like.

Everything was damp in that way only a public bathroom can be. The humidity weighed the air down, making it too heavy for the lazy fans overhead to move, to breathe. Heavy enough to muffle any cries for help.

I kept expecting someone to walk in. Interrupt us. I was certain someone would hear the screaming, would come in to take over proceedings.

I watched the door, but it never opened.

If anyone heard, they didn't bother investigating, and I don't blame them. It was late at night, a lonely space. It's a miracle that I ended up there myself.

"I think she's stuck. Is she stuck?"

The despair of labor was absolute and interminable.

She won't come out. She'll never come out.

I'm stuck here in some kind of purgatory as I wait for the pushing and pulling to end, but it never will. I'm only stuck in this moment.

My arms tired, the knees of my pants sopping up blood.

You were a surprise in more ways than one. One moment, pushing seemed impossible. There was no hope of you ever coming out. The next, your head was out and then, all at once, you were there.

A sweaty gasp of relief.

"Is she all right?"

I wasn't prepared for the blood. A sudden flood that crashed against the tile, making bright red rivers out of the browning grout. But this was a strange circumstance. I expect my own mother, who had only ever given birth in a hospital, had either never bled this much or never been forced to see it, sit in it.

I wish I could ask her now.

"Is she all right? Please can I hold her?"

There you were in my arms, weeping, crying. Not the only one in that lonely restroom doing so. Red and angry as a bee sting.

Cutting the cord was difficult. Physically disgusting but also a field full of new questions and second guesses. Was I doing it

right? Could it hurt you? Could it get infect-
ed?

In the end, you just have to do your best and move forward. That's what being a mother is all about. It was the first of so many decisions I would make.

"Can you please call an ambulance? Someone, please—"

The words slurred and dulled as they echoed off the tile.

You were beautiful. It was an ordeal, of course. We were both dirty and tired and crying, but I held you and knew you were the most beautiful thing I'd ever hold.

I've heard there's a chemical that releases in a mother's brain that bonds her to the baby right after, makes her forget all the pain from moments before. It's another one of those bits of information, passed down like a trade secret.

But I know that isn't all it is.

Because I took you from her, and my brain released all those same chemicals without the labor. No pain of mine, none of my blood on the floor. Yet I knew the second I held you that you were mine.

She was too weak to say goodbye, but I gave her a kiss on the cheek as a thank you. I left her bleeding, skin paling as I tucked you into my jacket. Cozy and silent as I took you the rest of the way back to your new home.

I'll wait a few days, maybe a week, before I take you to the hospital. No one will bother asking questions. A surprise baby; a home birth. They are both wonderful gifts no one will look at too closely.

If the neighbors hear you, they may cause trouble. We won't worry about them for tonight.

Besides, you've stopped crying already. Your red face now slack and peaceful against my chest.

I only need a few days.

And you will be quiet, won't you?

NOT LIKE THE SEAHORSES

S.E. Howard

"No way!" exclaimed a boy in the back of the Burkesville branch of the Wheeler County Library. No more than eight years old, he was one of a group of a dozen children, all seated criss-cross-applesauce around assistant librarian Phoebe Abrams for Saturday Story Hour. Phoebe wore a bright blue foam hat fashioned to resemble a seahorse's head to go along with the book she'd chosen to read that afternoon: *Friends and Family in the Deep Blue Sea.*

"No way," the boy said again. "You just told us boy seahorses have babies!"

The other kids giggled, and Phoebe lowered the book. "It's true," she said. "They carry them inside a special pouch in their bellies until it's time to be born. Then they open up their bellies and the babies all swim out, hundreds, even thousands at a time."

"That many?" another child asked, and when Phoebe nodded, they all chattered together excitedly.

"But they can't," the first boy insisted. "They're *boys.* Boys can't have babies!"

"How do they get inside the daddy's belly?" a girl asked.

"I… um, don't know," Phoebe said as from the main desk, Carrie shot her a glance, her lips pressed together as she struggled not to snicker. "I guess it must be magic."

....

"Magic, huh?" Carrie asked a short time later with a laugh. "Boy, you walked right into that one."

"Shut up," Phoebe said, pulling off the seahorse hat and slapping it playfully onto Carrie's head. "Next time, you're doing story hour."

"God, no," Carrie exclaimed. She'd been Phoebe's roommate during their freshman year of college and remained her best friend—her only one, really—as they now neared completion of graduate school. "I can't stand kids."

"Don't let Jasper's mother hear you say that," Phoebe teased and when Carrie groaned, she said, "Is she still pestering you about grandchildren?"

Carrie rolled her eyes. "The woman is relentless."

A month earlier, she and her boyfriend Jasper had married. Phoebe had been one of the bridesmaids and kept a picture from the wedding in a frame on her desk.

"You don't think you and Jasper will have kids?" she asked.

"I don't know," Carrie said, picking up one of the many pictures of Jasper off her own desk and studying it. "I mean, we've talked about it, sure, but his mom's ready for me to start popping out grandchildren left, right, and sideways, like one of your seahorses."

At this, still wearing Phoebe's hat, she puffed her cheeks full of air, and uttered a fish-like, "glub-*GLUB*" that made Phoebe laugh hard enough for Mrs. Fulkerson, the head librarian, to award them both a disapproving glare.

"How about you and Ryan?" Carrie whispered. "Do you want kids with him?"

Phoebe glanced at the other picture on her desk: a young man with dark hair and a broad smile. "Someday, sure," she admitted. "He'd make a great father."

Carrie scoffed and Phoebe frowned. "Why are you always so hard on Ryan?"

"Because he always acts like he's embarrassed to be seen in public with you."

"No, he doesn't."

"Like hell! How many times have I met the guy?" Carrie asked, then held up both hands, curled and cupped together to form a zero. "None."

"We've only been together a few months," Phoebe protested.

"Yeah, and in that time, I've never laid eyes on him," Carrie said. "He didn't even go with you to my wedding. Who blows off free food and booze like that?"

"He didn't blow it off," Phoebe said. "I've told you a hundred times. He was out of town. He travels for his job."

"Yeah, well," Carrie remarked, "Jasper thinks you've made him up. Just so you know."

....

Phoebe had loved libraries from the time she was young. Having grown up in foster care, she always found the familiar fragrance of books and the intimate confines among the shelves both comforting and welcome reprieves from her otherwise everyday uncertainty and loneliness. It had seemed only natural, then, that she'd chosen this for a living. With a bachelor's degree in library sciences under her belt and a master's in her sights, she hoped one day to become director at a branch of her own.

Preferably one that's far away from Mrs. Fulkerson, she thought now, as the head librarian caught her before leaving with Carrie for the day.

"I had several parents complain earlier," she told Phoebe. "About the book you chose for story hour."

"I don't understand," Phoebe said in surprise. "There's nothing inappropriate in the story. It's about animals that live in the ocean. In fact, last year, it won the Caldecott—"

"Did you speak with the children about reproduction?" Fulkerson cut in.

"Wh-what?" Phoebe choked. "No, ma'am, of course not. There's a line that talks about how daddy seahorses… er, I mean males, carry the babies during gestation. It's a biological fact, nothing obscene. One of the children had questions, so of course, I tried to explain. It's actually quite fascinating. The males have what's called a brood pouch in their abdomens. The females have an ovipositor, which they insert into the male's pouch, then deposit eggs to—"

"I don't need to know the details, Miss Abrams," Fulkerson snapped, "and neither do our patrons—nor their children."

Her eyes flashed and Phoebe clutched at the strap of her bag, abashed. "Yes, ma'am."

"I'm afraid you'll no longer be able to host the Saturday Story Hours," Fulkerson continued. "I'll also have to make a note of this incident in your personnel file, and the disciplinary action taken to address it. Otherwise, it could reflect poorly on the entire library."

"Yes, ma'am," Phoebe said again, shoulders hunched now, cheeks ablaze with color. "I'm sorry."

....

"That bitch," Carrie complained before tossing back a shot of Jose Cuervo. As expected, Phoebe had found her waiting outside when she left the library, and once Phoebe relayed what had happened, a wide-eyed and righteously indignant Carrie had insisted they leave right then and there for the nearest

Mexican restaurant, which happened to be running a two-for-one special on both margaritas and tequila shots. Phoebe stuck to the former, while Carrie had gone for the latter, and as a result, Phoebe was a lot less shitfaced at the moment than her friend.

"She's probably never been laid even once in her life," Carrie said, grimacing as she bit into a lime wedge. "She's so uptight, if anyone tried to fuck her, I bet their dick would come out a lump of coal."

Phoebe had stopped trying to tell her it was no big deal. After all, she should have anticipated that the kids would have questions. But Carrie didn't like Mrs. Fulkerson anyway, and it's not like she needed much, if any, excuse to gripe about her.

"Speaking of dicks…" Carrie planted both elbows on the table with enough force to slosh some of the tequila from the next shot glass. "Where the hell's Ryan? He should be here comforting you, not me."

"He's at home," Phoebe replied, "and I don't want to bother him."

"He's your *boyfriend*. He's supposed to support you."

"He does."

"How?" Carrie exclaimed. "He's always stringing you along, saying he's out of town on business…"

"No, he's not."

"… and he's never around when you need him. I'm telling you, the guy's either married, or he lives with someone. Either way, you're settling for being a side dish, girl. And you deserve to be the main course."

....

When she was in third grade, Phoebe had gone on a field trip to a local aquarium. Here, while her classmates had gawked over jellyfish and lemon sharks, she'd discovered the seahorse exhibit, watching them paddle around in their tank, their tiny fins fluttering, their tails hooked around leafy tendrils of seaweed. The tour guide explained that once ejected from their father's brood pouch, baby seahorses—each no bigger than an M&M—were on their own to survive, abandoned by their parents in the vast expanse of the ocean. Of the thousands that were born in each individual brood, only half a percent lived to reach adulthood. That was why they had so many offspring at a time and why, as soon as one brood had been released, male seahorses were impregnated again almost immediately by the females. The survival of the species depended on it.

As stark and cruel a reality as that had seemed, the tour guide revealed a softer, more tender side to seahorses, as well. They mated for life, the same brood pair procreating again and again. Even though the males and females spent most of their time apart, the pair bonds would come together for an amazing spectacle of courtship, where their tails would intertwine and they'd swim together, almost appearing to dance.

Watching the seahorses, Phoebe had felt a strange affinity. Then as now, she'd dream sometimes of a strange and terrible darkness. In these dreams—which felt more like memories to Phoebe, distant and nearly forgotten—she imagined herself floating in an endless black void, arms and legs outstretched, mouth agape, eyes wide. Millions of lights in clustered pinpoints were visible all around like distant stars, and ahead of her, bright and beckoning, a blue-green orb like the Earth. It was beautiful to her, but awful at the same time, because she was completely, utterly alone, drifting helplessly along like an untethered balloon caught in the breeze.

Was that how baby seahorses felt? she'd wondered. And if it was, did that mean she, too, might one day not feel like a castaway in her own skin? That she might find someplace, *someone* who felt to her like libraries always had—like home?

....

"I'm back," she called when she walked through the front door. Dropping her bag onto a table in the foyer, she shrugged off her coat and looked around the dark apartment.

"Ryan?" Phoebe walked down a short hallway toward the kitchen. "I'm sorry I'm late. Carrie made me go out after work for drinks. I hope you weren't worried."

As she spoke she opened the refrigerator door, then leaned down and grabbed a bottle of water. "Old Mrs. Fulkerson was in rare form today. She got onto me about reading a book at story hour to the kids."

Twisting off the bottle cap, she took a long drink, then nudged the refrigerator door closed with her hip before making her way to the adjacent dining room.

"It was a Caldecott Award-winner, at that. Can you believe it?" she asked, and when she turned on the lights, she saw him standing in the doorway between the dining room and bedroom. "Oh, my God! Ryan!"

She'd screwed heavy duty eye plates into either side of the doorframe, and through these, she'd secured chains connected to manacle cuffs around his wrists and ankles. She'd bought a ball gag online that kept him mostly quiet throughout the day, and luckily what little sound he was able to make had yet to alert any of their neighbors. She kept telling him she hoped she wouldn't have to use these things for long, just until he stopped trying to yell for help, or run away if she unshackled him.

He dangled heavily in his bonds but raised his head as she turned on the lights. His dark hair hung in his face, his eyes rimmed with heavy shadows, his lips cracked and pale around the edges of the ball. She saw dried blood on the corners of his mouth, caked and crusted on his chin, disappearing in the overgrowth of beard stubble accumulating there. He wouldn't let her shave him, shrieked if she tried to touch him, and she wondered—even worried—if he'd ever come to trust her again. Never mind love her.

Of course he will, she thought. *He's my soulmate. Just like the seahorses.*

"This wasn't supposed to happen yet," she said, hurrying toward him. He panted for breath, his entire body sweat-soaked and heaving. His abdomen looked bloated and distended, the skin shiny and slick, with stretch marks cutting ragged lines leading to and from his groin.

"I thought we had more time," she gasped, and when she clapped his face between her hands, he bared his teeth in the rubber flesh of the ball and yowled at her, shaking violently, desperately to dislodge her.

"I'm so sorry," Phoebe said. "I know you're hurting. Hang on. I'll help."

Whirling around, she raced back into the kitchen, then jerked open a drawer, shoving past utensils and measuring cups until she found what she needed. Grabbing the shears, she ran back into the dining room, then fell to her knees in front of Ryan.

"It's okay," she said, and when she touched the swollen, pulsating swell of his belly, he mewled. "I'll help you."

With one hand, she pushed the heavy bulge of his paunch up, just enough to see beneath, the stripe of scar above the tangled nest of his pubic hair. It had only barely started to heal, the stitches she'd placed still visible.

"Please be still," she begged Ryan, and he uttered hoarse, rasping noises as he shuddered with pain. Her hands shook, and she struggled to hold the scissors steady. "Please," she said again, blinking against tears as she took a chance and cut.

Moments later, when she managed to snip the last stitch apart, the incision fell open. She had a fleeting glimpse of red meat beyond the pale edges of his flesh, then, as they spread wide, a brown, thick, viscous fluid spilled out. It splattered onto the floor, dousing the front of her clothes, and when Phoebe looked down, she could see objects moving in it: tiny, wriggling, struggling things, each no bigger than an M&M, with no visible eyes, only pale, segmented flesh, flailing legs, and gaping mouths.

"Oh," she gasped, and Ryan must have seen them, too, because he uttered a low, warbling sound.

More and more of the creatures tumbled out from his belly, the puddle on the floor widening in circumference, glittering and glistening with reflected light. Soon, the entire dining room floor was flooded with oily, rust-colored liquid, teeming with a mass of hundreds, if not thousands of squirming larvae.

"Oh," she breathed again, scooping some between her hands. They were the most beautiful things she'd ever seen. She promised they would never be alone—not in that world, or any other. She and Ryan would make more of them. Before she stitched his belly closed again, she would press her mouth against the wound, let the stalk of her ovipositor harden and rise, protruding from her throat, pushing past his threshold again and into the dark, tight confines of his gut, their womb.

"I'll make more of you," she whispered. "And I'm never going to leave."

Not like her parents had left her, adrift among the stars. Not like the seahorses, she decided.

No, not at all.

THE QUICKENING

Emma Rose Darcy

PRESERVATION WAS GETTING THICK with child, and to that point, everything had been perfect. She was standing in the market, a basket of bread on one arm and one hand protectively on her round belly with the other, cheeks glowing with pleasure as a group of married women clucked around her like hens, when the shadow fell over them.

The other women fell away, and quick, because no one wanted to touch Lament Perry.

She carried the taint of rumor, and did herself no favors in town.

"I understand congratulations are in order, Mrs Barrowe," Lament said, but her tone was mocking. Her eye slid over Preservation's body with an eye that made her uncomfortable because it seemed so knowing. She had barely even spoken a word to this woman before; what reason did Lament have to act this way?

"Thank you, Mrs Perry," Preservation mumbled, her eyes down. "My husband and I praise God for the blessing."

"God had little to do with it." Lament took a step closer, clearly enjoying the stricken looks of the other women. She reached out and slid a hand, firm and awful in its confidence, over Preservation's stomach. "It is me you should thank. I am the one who got you with child, not God, not your husband either."

Preservation recoiled as the women around her burst into excited muttering to each other behind their hands. "You couldn't, that's preposterous. Please, don't listen to her. It is nonsense. We all know that can't be."

"I did it. I snuck into your house while your husband slept and I put that baby in you," Lament gloated. She seemed to take up so much space, her eyes and teeth shining so bright it made Preservation's eyes smart.

"Stop it, stop saying that," Preservation cried. Lament was drawing more attention now. People in the market were looking up from their business and listening. Rumours had persisted about Lament for as long as Preservation had been aware of her, but she had always considered it idle gossip, and beneath her. Why was she the target of this woman's cruelty?

"You think it is a human baby in your belly?" Lament leaned in close, her voice turning husky. "I am not so dull. A bouncing little boy or blushing girl might be all your husband might be capable of, but I can do better. It will be so exciting to find out, won't it?" She gave a ringing laugh, and walked on, tossing her glossy black hair like a girl. Preservation looked about her, into the horrified eyes of the people who had watched the exchange, and felt faint.

Preservation had a secret. She pretended she was without sin, as close to being without sin as any woman could hope to be, but she was actually very prideful. She thought she had the most handsome husband of any of the local women, and he had the largest hands. She had been very sneaky and checked sometimes if she got a chance to compare. She knew she had gotten lucky with Shephard, because he was gentle, and patient, and the only time he ever got angry was to hear another man raise his voice at someone smaller than he was.

It was true, she thought, as she watched him sitting by the fireplace, working on repairing some fiddling thing in his large hands, that he was as slow to boil in the bedroom as he was anywhere else. There was no chance of him exhausting her with children, though thankfully he'd not left her fallow either. She rubbed her stomach and tried to shake the feeling of unease the incident at market had left her with. She wouldn't tell him about what Lament had said. It was too strange.

When he slid into bed beside her that night he said, "I hear you crossed paths with Lament Perry today."

"So you know, then."

"Hmm. According to the blacksmith we shall be welcoming a little porcupine instead of a strapping boy. But the store clerk assures me it will be a black cat, which Lament will take as her familiar."

"Well, that's fine I suppose," Preservation chuckled. "At least he'll have work." It relieved her to joke about it, even though it felt close to blasphemy. She sighed. "What made her say it, do you think?"

"The same thing that drives anyone to cut down a neighbor in their joy," Shephard said, his voice soft and sleepy, unconcerned. "Envy."

As Preservation was falling asleep she felt the baby move. Usually this feeling brought her joy, because it meant that all was well. But that night, it felt strange. Was that the scrabble of tiny claws she felt?

At church, the people who they were ac-customed to sitting by gave them a wide berth. Preservation looked at Shephard, fear in her eyes, but he shook his head and gave her hand a pat. They sat through service with their heads held high. They would not give credence to gossip. It was easier to bear when he was with her though. Alone, the mut-tering and whispering behind her back was harder to ignore. It wormed into her ears and under her skin, like the twinges in her belly, which grew more persistent and sometimes stabbed her with enough force to take her breath away.

The final straw came when she was turned away from Virtue Capel's churn on the porch. All of the other women, sitting qui-etly, their work around them, watched with hooded eyes as she was sent away.

"But why, Virtue?"

"You know why," Virtue hissed. "Bad enough to lay with a witch in the dark of night, but then to parade yourself in front of us like a jezebel. To humiliate your husband by sitting in church like you did nothing wrong!"

"I did no such thing!" Preservation spluttered. "Why is everyone taking the word of someone they would not give the time of day to over mine?"

"Why would she lie?" Virtue lifted one righteous shoulder. "She has nothing to gain but her ungodly offspring. Go on, Preservation. Time will tell if you are innocent or not. If the baby is born human, we will have you back."

Preservation found that she could not sleep. The larger her belly grew, the ceaseless roiling of the baby kept her awake with terrified visions of what could be inside her. She imagined tiny devils with hooves and horns. Goat-legged horrors. Piglets with snake eyes and forked tongues. She rubbed her stomach and felt the answering shape of foot or hand or head, but she only shuddered. What if it was a serpent? A child that looked human at first but spoke with the knowing voice of an old man and told terrible unavoidable future tragedies.

Shephard grew exasperated and then frightened. She would not eat or sleep, and grew ragged and thin and pale. He left food by her bed and left each day, and groaned to find it untouched when he returned at night. He begged women he knew to have been her friends to sit with her and grew angry, in spite of himself, when they refused.

He went to see Lament Perry.

She opened the door of the strange little house she lived in, far away from everyone else, and laughed to see him.

"Hello, Shephard Barrowe," was all she had to say for herself.

"Why did you say that thing?" he asked, wretchedly.

"What thing?" She squinted at him. She didn't know what he meant until he recalled for her that day months before at the market. For he and Preservation it had consumed their lives every day since. For Lament, however, she had not given it a second thought.

"Oh, that. It was just a joke, Mr Barrowe," she laughed, and tossed her hair, just as she had then. "I don't know why I said it. I suppose I just felt like it. It's fun to get among the chickens sometimes, ruffle some feathers."

"You have to tell everyone it isn't true," he insisted, grasping her roughly by the arm. "They are shunning her. She'll lose the baby."

"I didn't know gossip could make a woman drop a baby," Lament snickered. She pushed his hand from her arm with equal force. "I suppose women were made of sterner stuff in the old days."

He went back home in disgust and did not leave again, even to tend to his own work, until the baby was born.

They all knew the baby was coming because the neighbors heard Preservation start to wail and sent their children out like scouts to spread the word. It wasn't long before a crowd was gathered like when they came together to sing psalms or raise a new cabin. They waited outside the Barrowe place, watching with gleaming eyes. The women exchanged knowing glances, and out of the earshot of the men whispered some of their own birth memories. Some of them good, some of them bittersweet. They had a fair idea of what Preservation was going through in there. If things had been different, one or two of them would be in there with her; it wasn't really right that it be Shephard alone. They knew that. *But,* they shivered with morbid fancy, *what if what came from between her legs really was a screeching black cat?*

It would really be something.

The excitement began to wear off. The glances the women exchanged shifted from knowing to concern. The men stamped their feet and chafed their hands together. Began to make comments about needing to get back home, they needed some sleep before they had to get back up to get back to work. Someone else would have to tell them how things turned out. They still did not leave. A fool could tell the sounds coming out of the cabin were wrong.

"It's been too long," one woman said.

"My cousin sounded like that when the baby was stuck," another said, from the back. "She died before they could get it out."

"Someone needs to go in and help."

No one moved, at first. They shifted around, and looked at each other, their faces guilty. They all remembered Shephard coming to their houses, begging them to go and sit with Preservation, to reassure her. That she was frightened. They hadn't gone. Not one of them.

Temperance Gosnall finally dusted her apron, heaved a heavy sigh and nodded that she would go in. But then they pricked up their ears, one by one, and realised that the night air had fallen silent. They turned, almost as one, as Shephard Barrowe opened his door. Ashen, he stepped out in front of them. The blood-stained cloth was balled up in his hands.

"Here," he said. "Pass your judgement."

He put the miserable little bundle on the ground and turned to go back inside. At the door he paused, to say over his shoulder, "You wouldn't sit with her while she suffered. Perhaps now you'll sit with her body."

A PIECE OF MY HEART

Ruth Anna Evans

"ARE YOU GOING TO do it?" Nick asked her this only three times since they found out. Jenna had no answer. Each time, she gave a little shake of her head and squeezed her lips together and turned away.

But now the clock was ticking. Literally. Her contractions were coming minutes apart, starting to bend her over, both hands on the mattress, insistent in their tightness. They weren't painful yet, but the thought of what was to come, after the baby was born, hurt more than the screwdriver agony that would twist her insides very soon.

"We need to decide," he said. "I need to know what to expect."

"Yes. No. Maybe. I don't know." She paused, and then for the first time since they had first found out about the decision they had to make, she asked him. "What do you want me to do?"

"I can't decide that. It's entirely your choice. But. I love you. I love you a lot. A lot a lot."

Jenna smiled. He always had been great with words. Their engagement had been a matter of, "Hey babe, would you, like, wanna get hitched or something?"

She had been thrilled. She was still thrilled. Marrying Nick had been the best decision of her life. Until now, it had been the biggest decision she'd ever made. But it paled in comparison to this.

The doctors had given them the news at the beginning of the second trimester. It had devastated them. At first, all they did was mourn. The days were dark and heavy. They didn't play music or read books or watch television. They just sat next to each other in their rocking chairs, holding hands sometimes. Going to work and coming home and not talking. They didn't go in the nursery, with its happy, pretty yellow walls and clean little crib. This was their first baby. This was supposed to be their first baby.

He was the one who pulled out of the fog first. He started researching. One day he was on the couch and Jenna dragged herself by to fix another cup of black tea and she saw him snap his computer shut, all the blood drained from his face.

"What is it?"

"Nothing."

"No, seriously, what?"

"It's nothing." He smiled at her, his face broken.

She walked over to him and held out her hands. He handed her the computer. She opened it and tapped in his PIN and looked.

Her hand flew to her mouth and the computer almost fell. He rescued it, closed it quietly, and set it on the coffee table.

"It's probably fake," he said.

"It didn't look fake."

"Why wouldn't the doctor have told us?"

"Can you imagine that conversation?"

"Yeah. You're right."

They didn't speak of it again for two months. But Jenna thought of nothing else, and Nick's long silences told her his mind was heavy with the choice too.

The pressure in Jenna's abdomen turned to a cramp, then a stabbing in her lower back. She was lowering her hefty body onto the bed when liquid gushed from between her legs.

Her stomach dropped so quickly she gasped for breath.

"It's time," Nick said. "We have to go." She nodded. He left the room and reappeared a moment later, diaper bag over his arm, and pulled her to her feet. She stumbled a bit and he steadied her.

"Okay," she said. "Okay, let's do this."

She wanted to be filled with joy, but there was no joy. She wanted to be giddy, anticipating seeing her child's face, but she knew it would be blue. And then she would never see it again. One way or another. So she didn't have anything to pull her through the pain.

At the hospital, they checked her in quietly, gently. The nurses had been briefed.

There was paperwork. A consent form. She filled it out but didn't sign it. No one said anything, just left it next to her on the little table with clattery wheels. Every so often, she saw Nick looking at it, between dabbing her brow with a cool cloth as she writhed her way through the contractions. She couldn't read his face. If only she could read his face.

"Don't do it," he said suddenly, as she panted between ripping contractions. "Please don't do it."

"It's our baby."

"I can't lose you."

"Who will I be if I let our baby die?"

"You'll be here. Please."

Another contraction hit and she arched her back until she felt her stomach would hit the ceiling.

When it was over, the nurse checked her.

"Time for the doctor," she said. "Do we need to go to the operating room?"

"Honey?" Nick asked, his voice very low.

"Yes," Jenna said. Nick buried his head in his hands.

The nurse's face stayed blank. "I'll let him know."

They had told Jenna that she would need to be under anesthesia before the baby came out, so they could make the transfer as quickly as possible. But to that, she said no.

"I want to see her."

"It may be too late if we delay."

"I want to see her. You'll just have to hurry."

She pushed her baby out on a cold metal table, feeling the rock-hard head rip through her burning vagina. At some point they had tried an epidural, but it hadn't worked and she didn't bother trying again. She wanted to feel it. She wanted to feel alive.

They handed her a grimy baby, limp and unmoving. She clutched her against her chest.

"We really have to move," the doctor said.

"Nick?" she clutched for his hand.

"I'm here. I love you."

They took the baby away and strapped it to the metal table next to her. She looked. The baby was so small. They slipped oxygen over Jenna's face—oxygen she wouldn't need much longer—and slid medication into her IV. She tasted cold pepper and was out.

"It's time for you to go on out," the nurse told Nick.

"I can't leave. I'm scrubbed. Please let me stay."

The nurse looked at the doctor. His eyes went soft above his mask and he shrugged a little and nodded. Nick folded his hands in front of him and bowed his head.

The doctor made a deep incision down the front of Jenna's chest. He attached a metal implement and cranked. There was a cracking sound. Tears dripped down Nick's face and splashed on the floor.

The doctor made some cuts and lifted the heart dripping from Jenna's chest. The baby was intubated, its little chest pumping. The doctor cut and cranked at the baby's chest and lowered Jenna's heart into the cavity.

He would leave the chest open while the baby grew. She should be big enough at a year old. They would keep her sedated until then.

Why couldn't they use a baby heart, they had asked the doctor, had asked the Internet, had asked each other. *Why did it have to be Jenna?*

Babies born without a heart, everyone told them, *reject every heart but their mother's.*

But it wasn't working. The heart was turning gray. Nick could see it from across the room. It wasn't pumping.

The doctor locked eyes with Nick.

"What do we do?" Nick said through tears.

"There's only one more thing to try," the doctor said.

"Well dammit, let's try it!"

"Your heart. I've never tried a father, but hypothetically it should work."

Nick paused. "She'd be an orphan."

"Yes."

"She'd live?"

"I can't promise that. We would try."

Nick looked at Jenna on the table, blood soaking out from between her legs, her chest butchered open.

He nodded.

They prepped him quickly, haphazardly, flipping his gown to open at the front, assisting him onto the cold metal table, dousing him with iodine before he was even out. He was numb, cold. They laid him down and put the oxygen on his face, the drugs in his veins. He blinked and he thought of Jenna. She must have been so scared. He looked at the baby, splayed on the table next to him. *We forgot to name her*, he thought.

Then he was out, and they snipped his heart from his chest and plugged it into his little tiny baby.

The heart pinked up.

It started to pump.

The nameless baby took a breath.

And she cried.

PROUD TO BE A MOTHER

C.J. Subko

My baby is now the size of a brussels sprout.

I eat and I shit more than I used to. It makes sense. I'm not really a woman anymore, but a vessel for this thing growing inside me. If it demands corn dogs dipped in ice cream, it's getting corn dogs dipped in ice cream. If it demands dirt and chalk, I surreptitiously go outside and huff down clods.

And then every morning I puke it all back up, part of me hoping I'll puke up the brussels sprout too.

It doesn't happen. The brussels sprout is rooted inside me, hitched deep within. Instead I stumble around all day chewing ginger for the lingering nausea and hover over my laptop doing my day job, because a mother's work is never done.

....

It had all started with a fling. We were both drunk, who knows, it was that weird kind of thing where I wasn't enthusiastic but I just wanted to get some before I got too old to be the kind of person who *could* get some. Anyway, he hadn't used a condom when he planted his seed in me but he did kiss me on the cheek after, sweet-like, gentle-like—and then I cried because I realized what had just happened, what it meant, and what it made me.

....

It was four weeks later I knew something was wrong. Or rather, nothing was wrong, because my underpants were clean, still. I hadn't been bleeding. For two weeks I hadn't been bleeding.

I was regular. I should have been bleeding.

In a drawn-up hoodie, I left my apartment, and it was like I could feel everyone's eyes; it was like they could sniff the taint on me.

I walked down to the drugstore and grabbed a box of pregnancy tests and three chocolate bars which were either going to be celebratory or conciliatory. I went up to the checkout counter.

The woman, older, grizzled, took one look at me and sneered as she checked me out. "Congratulations." Probably clocking my youth, my scraggly pink hair, my chipped black fingernails.

"For what?" I said dryly, playing it off like I had no idea she was talking about.

She sputtered something I couldn't understand, and I paid and grabbed my bag and got out of there, making my way with the dangerous package back to my apartment.

It doesn't take long to piss on a stick and wait for the symbols to show up; it takes an eternity. And after an eternity, my fate was sealed.

············

Back in the old days, I'd have gone to a doctor and "taken care of it." Shot up some chemicals or scraped it out of my uterus like stir fry out of a skillet. But this wasn't the old days anymore, and so my only option was to drive fifty miles to go to one of the few remaining doctors who still treated "women's problems."

It was an old, shack-like building made out of siding, with a plastic sign on the front that said "Dr. Brankovich."

I get out of the car and amble into the building.

The receptionist is a man, obviously. "Next," he says, and lets me back.

I heave myself onto a cold paper-covered table with two stirrups for my heels to splay my legs out.

Dr. Brankovich presses on my abdomen. Then he takes this metal rod and spears it into my vagina. I hiss at the pain, but he doesn't slow down. He doesn't become gentler.

The screen shudders to life.

"There it is," he says, pointing to a shape like a sprouting leaf. "It will grow and grow and grow. Healthy child."

I start to cry and he barks, "No crying, this is a good thing. You should be happy."

"I'm crying because I'm so happy," I lie.

I pay more than I can afford at the reception and then I get to my car and once I'm on the road I start to scream, scream, as loud as I can.

....

My baby is the size of a grapefruit.

It is beginning to grow proper leaves and vines. The tendrils of its vines push up against my stomach, creating curlicue patterns rounded against my pale skin. I touch them and they writhe and I scream. They move inside me, curling and uncurling against my stomach.

I go back to Dr. Brankovich.

"Where are the feet?" I ask. "Where are the little feet?"

Dr. Brankovich prepares the ultrasound and looks upon me with that enviable, disgustingly serene expression. "Some babies are different than others." He jellies my stomach and we observe the inside.

I gasp. It is a mass of tangles, like spaghetti, like hair.

"There," says Dr. Brankovich, "there are its vines and its leaves. It's growing along quite nicely."

He does not seem disturbed, not until I break down crying and shout, "Get it out of me!"

He tsks, "You know what that kind of talk could do. It'll be fine. You and your baby will be fine."

• • • • • • • • • •

I lose the next few months. Two? Three? My baby is a cauliflower. He is a cabbage. He is a butternut squash.

I am a corn husk stuffing myself with corn dogs and ice cream and dirt and chalk while the tendrils lash against my stomach, tap dance against my bladder. Sometimes my vagina leaks blood for no reason. The first time this happens, I hope to god I'm spewing out a malformed fetus but no, it's just tissue and blood, and I'm stuck as ever.

"Being pregnant isn't an excuse to slack off," my boss says, and doubles my work. I slash through it during the day and then at night I turn over every which way trying to sleep but my body aches, and the tendrils thrash in my stomach, and sometimes I think about ending it, but wouldn't that be worse?

....

It is six months since the conception. My baby is the size of a lettuce. My best friend and my sister have decided to throw me a baby sprinkle. It's the kind of shower you have when it's a second baby, or when you're poor.

Jen invites a few of her friends to round out the sad bunch. We have a cake that immediately sends me to the toilet to cough out breakfast, and a cheese plate I pick at with somewhat greater success.

"Come on," says Jen, "open the gifts!"

A little tear wends down my cheek. I guess I didn't expect there'd be gifts, in a situation like mine. Taking up the first box, I tear open the neutral yellow paper and open the box.

A lump sits at the back of my throat, and presses forward, pushing for sobs. It is a large, terracotta pot, with a bag full of potting soil. A starter kit in which to plant my baby.

"Thank you," I choke out, and I can tell Jen is pissed that I'm crying but whatever, it's not her day. "Thank you," I say, as I open up rubber gloves and a water can and trowels.

"Thank you," I say when all the presents are opened. "You've all been so kind."

There are games, afterwards. We play one with smushy candy bars in diapers where we have to guess which candy. It sends me to the toilet again. We play another that's all guessing games about me. Jen's friends are lost on the details, and no one does very well.

Finally, they all leave, Jen giving me a kiss on the cheek and a hug and a, "You're doing well" as she goes, but how the fuck would she know that I cry every night and shit myself every morning?

....

My baby is the size of a winter melon.

I am standing at the sink and I am holding a full bottle of weed killer. I read on the internet that this stuff is the best to kill any kind of plants, so you don't want to get it on your seedlings!

Unless you want to.

Can I do this? If I drink the whole thing, it will most certainly kill the baby inside me.

It will also most certainly kill me.

Have I reached this point?

Am I so trapped that the only way out is killing myself from the inside?

If Dr. Brankovich knew I was standing here like this, he'd have me locked up. After the baby was born, I could do whatever I wanted, but suicide of a vessel is capital murder.

I put my lips to the bottle. It tastes acrid and green.

Leaving it on the counter, I collapse to the floor and sob into my stomach; I can't even bend over to reach my feet. It's too late. I'm too stuck. I don't want to die. I just don't want to be this thing's mother.

....

I am sleeping, or half asleep, when a sharp rubber band of pain shoots across my crotch.

I wake up wet.

Fuck, fuck, my water's broken. I need help. I need to be at the hospital.

Ambulances aren't free, so I call Jen, who was also asleep, and beg her for a ride. She's a good sister; she's on her way.

While I wait, I am in agony. The contractions split open my vagina or my abdomen or I don't even know, everything down there just *hurts*. By the time Jen runs into my room, I am sweaty and screaming.

"Shit, how close are they?" says Jen.

"I don't fucking know!" I yell.

"Let's just get you to the hospital."

Throwing a blanket over myself to cover my fluids and my bare legs, I waddle with Jen towards her car and plop into the passenger seat.

Jen drives like a maniac. I black out a few times before we reach the hospital, where a gurney is waiting.

"Don't leave me!" I beg Jen.

"I have to park. I'll meet you in the room," she promises, and it feels like the last time I'll ever see her.

I blink, I black out, I am in a double room next to another pregnant woman who is shrieking and demanding an epidural. Should I get an epidural?

As though reading my mind, the male nurse says, "It's too late for that."

I am given a hot water bottle to tickle my stomach as the contractions lightning through my body, closer together now.

Dr. Brankovich comes in calmly, like I'm not about to die. "Dilation?" he asks.

"Seven centimeters," says the nurse. "Contractions about three to four minutes apart."

Dr. Brankovich grins. "Oh, it's close. Are you ready to be a mother?"

I sob and sob.

Dr. Brankovich puts my feet up on the stirrups and looks into my crotch which is tearing like tissue paper and bleeding, and he grins and says, "Don't push! We're not there quite yet."

It all happens so fast. Vines of the kudzu, thick green, thorny vines, force their way out of my vagina, tearing my delicate flesh as they whip out into the world and coil around Dr. Brankovich's neck.

"Help!" he tries to scream but it's only mime, for the kudzu has a stranglehold on him, his face is purpling, eyes bulging, the nurse is shrieking for help, for scissors, but the kudzu is too thick and strong.

And through the immense pain I am laughing, shrieking and keening laughing, because my baby is born, and for the very first time, I am proud to be a mother.

MOTHER EARTH AND THE TERRESTRIAL BIRTH

Jacy Morris

On a balmy May afternoon, the Earth's vagina manifested underneath Washington D. C., at the confluence of the Potomac and the Anacostia Rivers. It opened suddenly, the earth shaking violently, swallowing a hundred square miles of concrete, brick, and asphalt in the blink of an eye. The Washington Monument tumbled into the crack, followed by the Lincoln Memorial, the White House, and all the men and women who tried to keep America running.

The initial reaction was one of shock, and then, the people laughed and rejoiced. The religious pointed to the incident as proof positive of God's disdain for the United States of America.

Then the oligarchs got together. With time and money on their hands, they had enough capital to make their dreams come true, no matter how silly those dreams were. A race to plumb the depths of Mother Earth's birth canal began. They paid scientists, who shook their heads, then said they could do what the oligarchs wanted, even if it wasn't the wisest decision.

The world wanted to own that stretch of land. But how do you own a hole?

The bidding for what had once been the capital of the United States of America grew fierce, and the rich banded together to outbid each other, forming investment groups to be the first to explore the depths of our planet, to find out what was down there. The United States military had tried, sent drones down into the dark, rock-lined chasm, but none returned. "Too deep," they said.

An investment group led by a pharmaceutical company won out in the end, arguing that minerals and medicines might be found in the depths. They built a probe, massive, phallic-shaped, so much so that it put Jeff Bezos' spacecock to shame. They hung it from a helicopter, and then plunged it into the earth.

People all around the world tuned in, curious about this bottomless chasm. As the probe traveled deeper and deeper, the helicopter sunk out of sight, its lights and cameras sending back images for the scientific community to consume.

The people of the world leaned forward, except many of the world's women, who felt that the Earth should be allowed to have a vagina and not have it spelunked by man.

Those who stuck around witnessed something marvelous. The probe reached depths no human or living creature had ever been to. Many celebrated this new all-time low for humanity. The helicopter descended, its rotors coming perilously close to the edges of the vertical canal the deeper it went. The probe hit bottom seven miles into the earth. Its sensors strobed outward, pinging off walls of flesh-like rock, pink and wet with moisture. They tried everything, X-rays, laser, radar, sonar, and GPR. The data they received was disbelieved at first. But then actual scientists stepped in, pored over the information, and came to a consensus. Except for those fringe scientists who were scientists in name only and wanted to blame the slit in the Earth's surface on everything from aliens to God, everyone agreed.

The Earth—our Earth—was pregnant.

On late night TV, the hosts joked about who the dad might be. They made jokes about celebrities, politicians, reality TV stars, anything to get a laugh, because the truth—that no one knew—proved too frightening.

If the earth was pregnant, what was it giving birth too?

And that's where the world broke apart, where the consensus faded and molted into discord. Religious authorities insisted this was the birth of a terrestrial God. The pope insisted He had come to save them, to deliver them from the evil of Satan. Some claimed this was the next coming of Jesus. Others, doom and gloom types, insisted the Earth was giving birth to the anti-Christ.

The fear of those cry-and-die types spread, because fear is more contagious than logic, and these religious purists insisted the Earth's baby should be aborted. What if another full-sized moon popped out of there? What would it mean for the planet? For gravity? For the tides and the very systems that kept the world working?

The fear and rhetoric spread like wildfire, and the talking heads on the TV told the people what to think, and they thought it. In a stunning reversal, the church began to argue for an abortion. Others argued it was the

Earth's choice, and she had given no sign she wanted to have her pregnancy terminated.

Back and forth they argued. Radical fundamentalists dove into the birth canal with TNT strapped to their bodies, willing to die to take away the choice of the planet, but to no avail.

When the Earth's water broke, it did so with a violent wave of hot magma, gushing forth from the birth canal, spreading out over the eastern seaboard of the United States of America. Birth is a messy thing. When the magma cooled, the rough canal had been left shining, smooth and black. And then the Earth's vagina began to dilate, the chasm spreading, devouring more and more of the structures and roads man had built upon the Earth's body.

The contractions were even worse. They came days apart at first, but they grew stronger, toppling skyscrapers around the world. People died. Nothing taller than a single-story survived, and whatever actions humanity wanted to take were snuffed out by the reality of a broken world. People starved as food supplies dwindled. The power went out. No one could microwave their Hot Pockets. No one could DoorDash a pizza because the roads were all busted. All they could do was walk, and many made their way to the edge of the Earth's sex… to watch the end.

They rode the bucking Earth like surfers.

When the contractions came only a few minutes apart, and half the world had been crushed under their roofs, the Earth's progeny began its ascent, slowly, ever so slowly. Humanity could only wait and theorize.

What was coming?

When the Earth's child emerged, the people on the edge of the Earth's reproductive system watched, like people watching a solar eclipse. They lay on the ground, holding on for all they were worth as globular white forms emerged from the onyx-lined chasm. There were hundreds. They dripped magma so orange it looked red, as if blood rained from the sky. Their umbilical cords stretched for miles.

Humans smiled in awe at these new babies. New planets, maybe? Perhaps this was how the universe was born. No big bang, no string theory, none of that at all—just a celestial body birthing other celestial bodies. As the babies reached the limits of their umbilical cords' reach, the organic cables stretched and tore. The Earth's blood sprayed for thousands of miles, raining hot death along the entire Atlantic seaboard.

The newborn planets floated through the sky, and then the horrifying truth was revealed. As they awakened, attained some measure of motility, they descended upon the surface of their mother, feasting upon the humans like a human baby suckling at its mother's teat.

The last joke on late night TV came from a thin-faced man, from a mobile studio on the plains of Nebraska. "Well, we know who fucked the Earth, finally. All of humanity."

And Mother Earth took her revenge, her planetary babies scouring its tectonic skin. Where the sweet babes encountered humans, they descended like cartoon ghosts, their whiteness billowing in the air as they swallowed the people whole. Their acidic cores made quick work of human bodies—man, woman, or child.

There is no love like a child's love for their mother. And when the last simpering human had been transformed into a protein slurry, the Earth waved goodbye to her children, watched them bolt off into the cosmos, to begin the cycle anew.

THE DRY EARTH GIVETH

Amanda DeBord

DEAD DRY SHRUBS RUSTLED in the wind. Dry corn husks blew along in front of me. How old they were. How long it had been since corn had grown in these fields. A bone-thin hare scampered across the path. My mouth watered, but I didn't stop. Families used to feed granny women, maybe even give them a chicken for their services. I prayed the

Thornes would have something to fill my belly.

I arrived at the Thorne house and entered without knocking. The air in the two-room shack was cold and damp and stank like old dust, all mold and dry rot. Elizabeth, the Thornes' oldest surviving child, stared at me from behind tangled dark hair, wild-eyed and sunken-cheeked. She cowered over the table, her spoon plunging into a steaming bowl of stew. Something in the bowl moved. My stomach turned as Elizabeth returned to her meal.

A whimper from the bed stole my attention. Mary Thorne tried to sit up, tried to swing her legs over the bed, struggling against the hands and shushing of an old woman. That must be Elizabeth, Mary's mother. The little girl's namesake. The one who'd sent for me.

"Mother, I can't," Mary cried. "I can't do it anymore. I want to go back home."

"You ain't got a home, child," the old woman hissed. "You threw that away."

"Jacob will come for me," Mary whispered.

"After what you done? He ain't never coming back after what you done."

Mary wailed and fell back on the bed.

"Mother Thorne," I said, approaching the older woman. "Please. Go boil us some water."

"Granny!" Mary cried when she saw me. "Help me. I don't want to … I can't …"

Something moved under the blankets and she drew her feet up, covering her ears and closing her eyes.

The bed stank. The blankets stank. Despite the cold, sweat mixed with tears rolled down Mary's pale cheeks.

"Quiet now, child. You know it's got to happen. We've got to get this baby out. You've done this what, five times now? You and Jacob have three fine children, and you're going to have one more. None of that crying and begging is going to stop what's coming."

"That ain't no baby of Jacob's," Elizabeth hissed from the kitchen. "The last one weren't, neither."

"The last one? Baby Molly? Why of course she was Jacob's. Her eyes looked just like his. Where is the little mite?" I asked, wiping Mary's brow.

"He took her with him," she sobbed, "when he saw it."

"Saw what?"

"Granny, the babies are already coming out. There were two yesterday. I think another one this morning."

"You think? What do you mean, you think? Speak plain!"

"It got away before I could see it. Mama took the first two away, but I felt them. They were … they were …"

She gasped and threw her head back on the bed and screamed, digging her heels down into the mattress. She arched her back like her poor spine would break. "Another one's coming!" she wailed.

Elizabeth the elder and Elizabeth the younger crowded the doorway, the child's mouth brown and wet with stew.

"Get the girl out of here!" I shouted as I pulled the quilt up over Mary's knees. "She shouldn't see this."

"She already seen't it," the old woman said. "And good it was, too. See what happens when one goes cavortin' with animals."

"I didn't …" Mary grunted, but didn't finish. She clenched her jaw and bore down. I reached for her leg, ready to push back and help her get traction, but before I could, the small wet child slid out onto the stained mattress. It was still.

"Get me a towel, woman! And that water! And …" The baby started to move. It kicked a soft red leg out from its body. "It's alive," I breathed. Before I could continue, the baby kicked its other leg and I saw it wasn't a baby at all. Its feet were too long, its legs bent in the wrong places. What I'd thought were tufts of hair perked up, tiny oval-shaped ears growing from the top of its head. A matted white tail poked from between its hind legs.

A rabbit. A wet and bloody rabbit stirred to life there on the mattress between Mary's legs. Full grown, it looked well-fed and healthy.

As I watched, it sat up and began grooming itself.

Elizabeth the elder muttered a prayer while the little girl came forward with a towel. I reached for it, at least wanting to clean Mary up, prevent childbed fever, but the girl grabbed the rabbit by its hind legs, wrapping it in the towel as it shrieked and kicked. She carried it away to the kitchen as Mary sobbed. I heard a wet *thunk* and the rabbit was silent.

"My baby …" Mary whispered as her body went limp. "Please let me keep one …"

I sat by Mary's bedside long into the night. I'd forbidden the Elizabeths from reentering the room, threatening them as only an elderly granny woman could. They respected me. I'd delivered the younger girl and even attended to the old woman in her time. They sat in the dark kitchen, silent, while I waited for Mary to wake up.

As she did, she reached out, tears forming again when her hands found nothing and her eyes opened to see only me at her bedside. "Granny …" she whispered. "What's happening to me?"

"You tell me, child," I said softly, not wanting to draw the attention of the women in the kitchen. "You seem to know."

"There are animals coming out of me. We've got no more animals in our pens, but they're coming out of me. None in the fields. Not even in the barns. The famine took them all. This place used to swarm with vermin after we took in the harvest. We had the fattest tom cat in the village. When was the last time you saw a tom cat, Granny?"

"It's been a while, dear," I admitted. "We're all hungry."

"I'm so hungry, Granny." Mary whispered. "All I ever think about is food. Stew. I went out in the field and laid down in the dirt and prayed for a rabbit to eat. Something for Jacob to catch. I was so hungry."

"I pray, too, Mary. Father Joseph tells us …"

"Not like that. I prayed like we used to. Like they tell us not to no more. I took up the dirt, and I rubbed it on myself … in myself …" She blushed. "I prayed to the animals that they'd bring themselves to us. I made the old signs with my fingers. And I said that word. You know the one. I was so ashamed, but I was so hungry. I looked up and they was watchin' me. Three rabbits and a deer, just standin' there. And I felt it inside me."

"Mary, that's just …" I wanted to tell her it was superstition. That Father Joseph told us it was, that the Lord in Heaven would give us all the bread and the stew we needed. But I was hungry, too. I'd wanted to do what Mary had done, had sat on my hands to keep them from making the sign myself. I'd been afraid.

Something moved underneath the quilt and I raised it again to see a soft pink nose twitching.

"Can't I keep just one of them?" Mary pleaded as she reached down between her legs to stroke its brown fur. "They're my flesh, after all."

I heard a dry cough in the doorway. The young girl stood there, her chin wet with saliva. "Go away, dear," I scolded. "Let your mama rest."

"Then come, Granny," she said. "Come eat."

I ate for a long time. I sucked rabbit meat from the bones in my bowl, and the juices dripped down my fingers as I heard Mary gasp again from the bedroom. I would go to her after supper. I closed my eyes and imagined green fields again. Full larders. Full bellies. I made the secret sign with my hand as I lifted another spoonful to my mouth.

When I opened my eyes again, I peered through the flickering candlelight into the bedroom. Mary smiled at me, whispering a soft lullaby as she lifted a spotted fawn to her breast.

I stood, smiling back at her and feeling a long-absent strength return to my bones. How long had it been since I'd tasted venison?

"Let us keep the feast," I said.

LITTLE FOX

Tory Favro

Timmy laid down quietly in bed. The night was silent other than the twin thumps in his chest. The little seven-year-old was scared of the dark but Mummy had put the night light on in the corner of the room. The corner where there was a bed that no one had ever slept in. It was for sleepovers, Daddy had told Timmy with a wink, suggesting the little boy had fun in store for him. Timmy knew better, ever since he had seen Mummy's diaries.

The empty bed was not for friends. Timmy had none, other than Mummy and Daddy, who were his world. Timmy had learned that the bed had been made for his brother many years ago but never slept in. Nor would it ever be. The bed had been made for…Little Fox.

Timmy felt his chest pound in the night, it was hard to breathe and every time he felt his heart thump, there was a hard echo in his chest.

Ka-Thump - Thump!

It was enough to make him stay awake all night. He had shadows under his eyes. Mummy and Daddy tried to help him sleep but with that second thump he couldn't settle down.

Ka-Thump - Thump!

"Little Fox, is that you?" Timmy asked the second beat in his chest. He placed his tiny hands over his heart and talked to the little boy who had never been. His brother. His Vanishing Twin. Timmy had seen the pictures in the diary. Two baby boys inside

Mummy's tummy. Two. Not one. But only one had come out. Him.

Timmy.

Ka-Thump - Thump!

Timmy had taken to talking to Little Fox ever since he saw the photos and under-stood why Mummy was so sad. He knew that Mummy loved him, Daddy too, but they were so quiet all the time and would not let him play on the second bed.

"That's for sleepovers, fella," Daddy told him as he gently lifted Timmy off the pristine bed that Mummy fixed every day, brushing the dust off.

It was about nine months ago that Timmy had found out about Little Fox. His Brother. That HE ate. It was about nine months ago that Timmy had started eating a lot. He grew taller and taller as you do at his age, but Tim-my also grew…

Fatter.

Thicker.

Mummy was the first to call him her chub-by bubby. Daddy had laughed but told her to keep that to herself. He had a sip of his drink.

Daddy had nighttime drinks, and sometimes he was funny, but most of the time he was sad. Timmy loved him so very much and he knew that Daddy loved him too. He knew that Mummy did as well but her love for Little Fox was there also. Timmy knew that for some reason, Mummy thought that Timmy WAS TO BLAME for Little Fox not being in the world. Timmy did not understand that, but he knew that Little Fox was special to Mummy and Daddy and therefore should be special to him.

So he spoke to Little Fox and as he spoke, his belly grew and grew. He knew it was a way that Little Fox could talk to him. He did not like being called fat though. Not one little bit. He was a brother and that was all. The kids at school avoided him unless the teacher made them talk to him. That was okay. He felt the roundness of his belly and knew that it was not from food like the kids teased him about.

Ka-Thump - Thump

His skin sometimes hurt when he touched it. It was tender though he was too young to know that word. He ran his hands over his belly. It felt like a basketball and at times it hurt. The kids at school teased him, and that hurt him a lot. He didn't care, well a little bit of him did. But he was being a good brother.

Ka-Thump - Thump

Sometimes in the night when all was dark, he felt a tightness in his stomach and chest. It was hard to breathe. Mummy gave him a puffer to use.

"Just two puffs sweetie, pull it deep into your mouth," she said. Most of the time, it worked. Tonight it didn't. Tonight his tummy hurt and he could not breathe right at all. Timmy tried to call out for Mummy or Daddy but the tightness stopped him. In his mind, he knew that it was Little Fox, moving about and wriggling through Timmy's insides.

"Hello?" Timmy gasped into the darkness. The shadows did not answer with more than a muffled sound that Timmy thought was a scream like his Nan made before she was hit by a truck. *Ka-Thump - Thump.*

He felt his tummy go soft and flat. It was like a balloon being let loose after too much air had been pushed in. It hurt. Timmy tried to call out to Mummy and Daddy but the pain stopped him. The pressure in the little boy's chest was too much. He thought he might pop.

Then he could not breathe.

Something was moving up from his belly. Something furry. Slender. Something that had taken its time and chosen right now to welcome itself into the world.

He was choking. Timmy was choking on the thing that was crawling out of his gut. Instinctively he knew it was Little Fox. His brother. His breath was ragged to the point of non-existence. The lump was passing from his stomach to his throat now; it burned and hurt so very much. It felt like his neck was too big for his body. Timmy felt claws work their way up his throat.

Little Fox, this hurts so bad, he thought out aloud as the claws climbed up his throat. *Can you hurry up?*

Timmy threw his head back. The pain was unbearable now, but his throat was blocked by Little Fox. No way Mummy or Daddy would hear him now. He lifted his hands to his mouth which was being forced open by whatever was crawling out of him. His probing fingers ripped ginger fur from his mouth. He felt a claw reaching for the chill air of his bedroom. The world was fuzzy as his throat constricted and did not allow air to pass from him.

Ka-Thump - Thump!

The scrabbling inside his tummy hurt so much. More than when the doctor gave him a needle that one time. It felt like sharp nails were moving inside of him. Timmy's jaw made a weird snapping noise and fell downward. He wished he was asleep and dreaming, it hurt so much!!!!

That's it! Maybe he was dreaming and when it hurt too much he would be allowed to wake up. Maybe when he woke up, he would have a brother and Mummy would love them both so very much! *Crack!*

Through tears, he could see that Little Fox was climbing out of his broken mouth. His baby teeth were barely hanging onto his gums as his brother used his claws to force his way from Timmy. A snuffling snout appeared, then two dark eyes looked about at the small bedroom into which Little Fox had been born. He had waited a long time to see Mummy and Daddy, but no one had believed in him. No one until Timmy had seen that picture and started talking to him.

Little Fox had felt himself grow in his brother's tummy. It was warm and soft and just right for a Little Fox like himself. Now, though, Timmy was not big enough to hold Little Fox and it was time to come out. Timmy was wet and red and Little Fox could tell that he had hurt his brother rather badly and for that he was honestly sorry. His back legs left Timmy's mouth and he stood on his brother's chest looking down on his broken face.

He licked some of the blood from Timmy and tried to work his jaws. He was changing already and had only one chance to be with Mummy and Daddy again. He could feel the change happening and knew that little boys didn't eat each other. But a Little Fox could eat whatever he wanted.

Timmy's eyes widened as Little Fox dove at his face with his jaws wide open. *Chomp Chomp Chomp*. He tried to stop Timmy hurting, honestly he did, so he bit as fast as he could, swallowing that little boy up. As Timmy had once eaten him in Mummy's tummy. *Crack Crack Crack*. His powerful jaws and teeth worked through his brother as they became one for the second time in their short lives, until Timmy was no more, asleep inside Little Fox's stomach. Little Fox felt really tired, his bones hurt and his skin stretched out, becoming a little boy, about eight years old, looking a lot like the boy who until seconds ago had called this place his bedroom. He cried out, a human sound as the last of his snout and fur disappeared into pink-white skin.

All that remained of Timmy was his voice and Little Fox decided to keep that. He cleaned up all the red wet and tidied the bed and settled in to sleep.

Daddy ran down the hallway and threw the door open, his shadow large on the carpet.

"Timmy? You OK, son?

Son! Little Fox loved the sound of that. He cleared his throat of the last pieces of meat and spoke out loud for the first time. In the voice of his brother.

"I'm OK Daddy. Must have been something I ate."

THE BABY STOPPED CRYING

Paul Avery Tindol

AT first, ABE FOUND the silence to be a relief.

Thank God, he thought as he closed his eyes, the world around him already fading out. Sonny had been crying pretty much non-stop for the first couple of weeks after Abe brought her home from the hospital. Those moments Sonny would sleep were his only chance to nap as well, even though he rarely got more than an hour at a time anymore.

Before he could completely drift off, he heard a low creaking sound, maybe a cabinet door opening, maybe footsteps on the loose board next to the coffee table in the living room. Maybe it was some missing part of the recurring nightmare he had found himself having, a detail he'd finally catch onto this time.

A few minutes later, Abe opened his eyes, unable to actually fall asleep due to his worked-up nerves. Then he thought about how the quiet had lingered for *too* long. Now it was so unbearably heavy, hovering in the air like a swelling rain cloud.

Something is wrong.

....

After his wife died, Abe knew the road ahead of him would not be an easy one. He was already worried about being a good enough father back when Cass was the one buying all the baby books and planning the registry.

He was never prepared to do this without her.

Truth was, Abe didn't even know that he *wanted* to be a father without her, his thought being that the child would probably be better off being raised by some healthy, stable couple looking to adopt. His family certainly wasn't an option.

Abe's employer gave him two months off work to recover from his loss and spend time with his child. He figured he should have been grateful for that, but the truth was that he was terrified of being alone with the baby all day.

He found that not only was it difficult, but that he was *terrible* at raising a newborn. No matter what he did, it seemed he couldn't get his daughter to stop crying. She hardly ever slept, especially at night. When she did get her periodic naps, and Abe also got a chance to momentarily nod off, he always drifted back into the same nightmare.

He's in the hospital room on delivery *(death)*

day and the walls and the lights and the scrubs and the doctor's mask and his gloves are all blinding white. Cassandra is pushing, grunting, and groaning, the veins swelling and popping out of her neck, her face blood red, until she lets out a shrieking scream.

It shakes the world and then the white walls and chrome machines around him start to shift and spin.

"She's almost here," the doctor assures his wife before turning to Abe with a twisted grin that hardly seems appropriate for the circumstances. "Get ready to catch her," he tells Abe then gestures down between his wife's legs.

Her screams grow louder as she crowns. Abe watches this happen as he lowers himself and the doctor places a cold hand on his shoulder, laughing maniacally, as Abe sees that the baby's head is misshapen.

It's supposed to do that, Abe remembers hearing. Something about the bones in the skull overlapping, making it easier for the head to pass its way through the birth canal.

And in *that* moment of trying to recall what he'd learned about the birthing process, he realizes that his wife is no longer screaming.

He looks up and Cass is completely still, her mouth open, one side of her bottom jaw hanging much too low to not be broken. Her eyes are rolling back into her head and becoming as white as everything else in the room around her.

"Everything is fine," the doctor assures Abe as blood and birth spews from her open legs, and sprays him and everything else in the room until it's all the colors of slimy, wet peppermint. The doctor continues laughing and slaps his blood-soaked hand onto Abe's drenched shoulder. "This is all part of the process, kid. How do you think you got here?" He snatches Abe's wrist quickly and forces Abe to touch the child hanging halfway out of his wife's lifeless vaginal canal and still crawling its way out as the bones in the child's head shift back into their normal places.

"See," he says. "Everything is completely fine." The gore-coated baby growls as the doctor guides Abe's hand over her soft wet cranium, where he can feel the fragile bones in her skull still moving back into place.

"That's a healthy baby girl," the doctor continues.

Abe looks back up to his wife in terror, already forgetting that she's dead, and reliving it again as he sees how much further her corpse has deteriorated. Black rings lay heavy around the glaring whites of the back of her eyes. The face that was straining red only a moment ago, now a bruised purple. Her jaw hangs even lower and the top row of her teeth begin to fall out like rain drops, one at a time as the growling child claws and swipes the rest of its way out of his dead wife.

....

After tonight's nightmare, Abe had already given his daughter another bottle after waking, and she was already crying ten minutes later. He laid there listening to the crying, asking himself why nothing seemed to work—when the crying finally stopped.

Thank God, he thought.

But after failing to fall asleep, Abe sat up to see the black silhouette standing over Sonny with its long black hair dangling over the edge of her crib. When his eyes traveled down the thing's body, he saw that its feet weren't touching the floor.

It was *hovering* over the crib.

His heart was in his throat and he tried his best to speak, but the words wouldn't come out.

Then Abe heard an unfamiliar sound that was music to his ears.

Instead of crying, Sonny cooed—like she wasn't *just* content, but happy.

The figure turned its head slowly in Abe's direction, but he still couldn't see her facial features. In a soft, soothing voice like velvet it said, "Lay back down, Abe. Sleep. I'll take care of her. Don't you worry."

Abe didn't know what to do. His body was at a point where it was going to crash hard, whether he wanted it to or not. The quiet was so—he collapsed back down into the mattress and was out like a rock.

The following morning he woke feeling the most rested he had since Sonny was born—and without having had that tormenting nightmare again.

Everything was fine for the most part the next day. Sonny didn't get fussy again until right around nine the following night, which went on for at least an hour before he sat her back in her crib and laid down to take a breather.

Then she stopped crying and the room suddenly felt twenty degrees colder.

Abe already knew what he was going to see before he sat up to look over to Sonny's crib.

This time the hovering figure, instead of telling Abe to lay back down, *asked* him if that's what he wanted.

"Would you like me to take care of her so that you can sleep?"

Despite the tears running down his cheeks, Abe reluctantly nodded and let his head hit the pillow.

Now every night when she starts crying the shape in black comes to soothe her.

And Abe lets it.

Its curvy features appear to be feminine, but Abe's not entirely sure it was ever human. But he had been sleeping so much better.

He *felt* so much better—until last night, that is.

During her most recent visit, after Sonny was sound asleep and Abe had also drifted off, he opened his eyes to a black cloud of smoky features resembling a woman hovering above his bed.

Her eyes were much too big, like over-sized, cute cartoon animal eyes. Her mouth hung open in an unnaturally wide smile, but he couldn't see any of her teeth. None of the parts of her face—her eyes, nose, or mouth—none of that seemed to stay in the same place. Instead, they kind of floated around like hollow objects in dark waters.

Then she spoke to him.

"You know how this ends," she said. Her voice was so soft.

Soothing.

"She is going to recognize me as her mother—and I will be."

Abe closed his eyes tight, unable to keep looking at her ghastly features. Then he felt the soft, cold tips of her fingers brush his cheek.

"What will she ever need you for?"

Before Abe could think of an answer, Sonny began to cry again.

"Would you like me to take care of her?" she asked softly. "Just say yes, once more."

Tears poured down Abe's cheeks in long streams as he nodded and waited for the silence.

STILLBORN

Sheri White

Erin put a forkful of cake into her mouth. The sweet pink and blue icing oozed between her teeth, making them ache, but she didn't care. She could barely taste the cake anyway, nor could she hear the happy chatter of moms and moms-to-be around her. This month's pregnancy test wasn't even needed this morning. Her period started while Erin was in the shower, clots dropping from her body and splattering on the tile before being sucked into the drain. Erin had been so sure she'd have her own happy news to share at her best friend's baby shower today. Instead, she was cramping and bleeding and trying not to cry.

They were celebrating the impending birth of Jenna's third child—her first little girl. Erin and her husband Alec had been trying for two years now to have a baby. They had both been tested; they shouldn't have been having so much trouble conceiving. Yet they remained childless.

Erin put her paper plate down on the coffee table. She couldn't finish the dessert. She just wanted to go home and sob. She looked at the women around her, in various stages of pregnancy, and pictured them all miscarrying, bloody and slippery fetuses plopping onto the floor from between their legs, little limbs flailing about as they died.

Jesus, what's wrong with me? That's fucked up.

"Hey, Erin! How's it going?" Abby, Jenna's younger sister, sat down next to her. She sported her own pregnancy bump, her first.

Erin forced a smile. "Everything's fine. So, when are you due?"

"In about four months. Bobby and I are so excited. We've even picked out names and furnished the nursery." She rubbed her belly and beamed, glowing as only a pregnant woman can.

Erin's smile faltered. "That's great. I'm really happy for you."

Abby was so wrapped up in her joy that she didn't notice Erin's lack of enthusiasm. "So, when will it be your turn? It would be so much fun for us all to raise babies together."

"Oh, I don't know. Soon I hope. Hey, will you excuse me for a minute?" Erin managed to get to the bathroom before she broke down in tears. She clutched her stomach, her uterus convulsing and cramping. She could feel the blood and mucous trickling past her tampon. She grabbed her purse on the way out of the bathroom and discreetly left the party.

....

"So how was the shower, babe? Did you have a good time?" Alec stroked Erin's long hair as she sat at the kitchen table with a glass of wine.

"Awful. Just like I knew it would be. I mean, I'm happy for Jenna and everything, but she's on her third baby and I can't even have one! It's just not fair." A sob escaped her throat. Alec leaned down and put his arms around her.

"I'm so sorry, babe. Are you sure you don't want to go for the in vitro option? We have enough in the bank to give it a try."

She turned around to look at him, and shook her head.

"But we shouldn't have to! There's nothing wrong with us. Why can't we have a baby like everybody else? I want one so badly, Alec." A tear rolled down her cheek, breaking Alec's heart.

"I'm crampy. I'm going to go upstairs and take a hot bath." She walked towards the stairs, defeat evident in every step she took. Alec watched her go, his own sadness matching hers.

·········

Steam rose off the water in the cool bathroom. The hot water relaxed Erin, relieving her cramps a bit. She felt peaceful for the first time all day. Then she coughed, hard, and felt her body expel another clot. It rose to the surface of the water, tendrils of blood snaking towards Erin. In a sudden fit of rage, she picked up the bloody ball and smashed it against the bathtub wall. It popped as it hit the tile, and blood sprayed the bathroom.

....

A few weeks later, Erin was holding Jenna's baby girl in the hospital. Jenna lay against her pillows, looking exhausted but happy. Flowers and balloons decorated the room.

"She's beautiful, Jen."

"Isn't she? She has her daddy's eyes, I think."

"You're so lucky. Oh! What's her name?"

"Hannah. I know it's kind of old-fashioned, but we named her after my grandmother."

"It's a sweet name." Hannah started to cry, and Jenna held out her arms. She undid her gown and put the baby to her breast.

"Look, I've got to go, Jenna. Call me when you get home, okay?"

"Sure." Jenna didn't even look up; she was intent on her new baby. The sound of Hannah suckling followed Erin out to the hall. She practically ran to her car.

....

Erin sat on the toilet seat, a big grin lighting up her face. She looked at the test stick again, just to make sure. Two lines. Positive.

"Well?" Alec stood in the doorway. He could tell by the look on his wife's face that they finally had good news.

She jumped up and threw her arms around Alec's neck. "We're going to have a baby! Finally!"

....

Erin couldn't stop smiling for days. She saw babies everywhere she went, and cooed at them, knowing it wouldn't be long before she had her own child to hold in her arms. She even visited Jenna and her kids, and was able to enjoy them instead of getting wracked with jealousy.

Her OB/GYN gave her a clean bill of health and prenatal vitamins.

Morning sickness hit her at about six weeks, but she didn't even mind that. She'd heard an old wives' tale that said the sicker a pregnant woman got, the healthier the baby was. That was fine with her. Alec held her hair back every morning while she vomited the previous night's dinner into the toilet bowl, then gave her crackers and ginger ale when she got back into bed. She worked from home, so she didn't have to worry about getting to work while feeling so ill. Life was truly good.

....

Erin was seven months along when she woke up in the middle of the night, knowing something was very wrong. She ran to the bathroom, and watched, horrified and scared as blood oozed down her legs and puddled on the floor. A powerful cramp doubled her over in pain and she called for Alec before passing out.

....

"I'm so sorry, Erin," Dr. Matthews said. "We're not going to be able to save the baby. We won't know what happened until we perform an autopsy. But for now, we'll deliver the baby by Caesarean section tomorrow morning."

Erin sobbed, tears streaming down her face. Alec held her, helpless and numb. Dr. Matthews opened his mouth to speak, then shook his head instead. He patted Erin's hand and walked out of the hospital room.

"Alec, I don't think I can go through this. Is she really dead? Maybe they're wrong! I mean, I hadn't felt her kick in a few days, but I thought she was just crowded in there, or sleeping. If I had only known, maybe she could've been saved!"

"Honey, don't. The sonogram showed there was no heartbeat. She's probably been dead a few days."

"Don't say that!" Erin screamed. "That's our baby you're talking about!" She couldn't bear the thought of carrying a dead baby inside of her body.

"Okay, okay. I'm sorry. But you have to get strong, babe. Please."

Erin buried her face in her hands and sobbed, her body shaking. "I can't, I can't."

The nurse came in with a syringe. "This will help her sleep. The doctor ordered it for her." She administered the sedative. A few moments later, Erin was asleep.

....

The following day Erin was prepped for surgery.

"I want to be awake when they deliver her. Don't put me to sleep."

"I don't think that's a good idea, babe. Just let them put you out, and then this will all be behind us."

"No! I want to see my baby. I *have* to see her. Please. It won't be real unless I do."

Alec rubbed her back. "Okay, babe. Whatever you need."

···•·•·····

The anesthesiologist walked in the room. "Hi, Erin. I'm going to give you the epidural. It's only going to hurt for a minute, then you'll be numb below the waist."

He had Erin lean over, Alec holding her tightly. He sterilized the area, then inserted a needle into her lower back. She bit her lip to keep from crying out. He taped the needle to her back.

"Okay, everything's good. In a few minutes, you won't feel anything from the waist down. I'll see you in the delivery room."

Erin lay back on the pillows, crying softly.

"Did it hurt, babe?"

"Did it hurt? Are you fucking kidding me? What doesn't hurt right now? My heart is *breaking*, Alec. A needle in my spine doesn't even register."

Alec could do nothing but look at his wife helplessly and hold her hand.

···•·•·····

"Okay, Erin. You're going to feel a little pressure here, but no pain." Erin felt like she was being unzipped as the scalpel traced a red streak across her bikini line. She could feel her flesh being spread apart. Then there was a tugging sensation as Dr. Matthews lifted the baby from her womb.

"Are you sure she's dead, Doctor? Are you sure?"

"I'm sorry, Erin. She's dead. She's obviously been dead for a couple weeks."

"I want to see her."

Dr. Matthews nodded, having been through this before. He cut the umbilical cord and handed the baby to the nurse. She wrapped the baby in a blanket and handed her to Erin.

The baby was gray, her skin mottled and her lips blue. Erin cradled the baby in her arms and kissed her on the cheek. The baby was still warm from being inside her. Tears ran down Alec's face as he watched his wife.

"Isn't she beautiful, Alec?" She snuggled the baby against her breast.

Alec nodded and stroked the baby's face with his finger. He didn't trust himself to speak.

The doctor removed the gray, brackish placenta and stitched Erin up. She could feel the epidural wearing off now that the anesthesiologist had left.

"Erin. I'm sorry, but we need to take her now." Dr. Matthews held his arms out.

"No. Please let me hold her for a while. I need to say good-bye."

Dr. Matthews patted her arm. "Okay, but only for a few minutes." He beckoned to the operating team to clear the room. "I'll be back shortly. I'll prescribe some pain killers for you as well." He turned to Alec. "Can I talk to you out in the hall? We have some arrangements to discuss."

Together they left the room, leaving Erin alone with the baby.

....

"Hey, little one. I'm your mommy. Your name is Olivia." She stroked the baby's gray cheek, gently running her finger down

Olivia's cooling skin. "Oh, you're chilly. Mommy will fix it." Erin pulled the blanket tighter around the baby, making sure her little feet were covered.

"Oh, God! You can't be dead, you can't! I've waited for you for so long!"

She held the baby close to her chest, rocking back and forth.

Mommy.

Erin stopped rocking. There was no way. She couldn't have heard that.

Mommy.

Erin looked at her baby. Olivia's eyes were still closed, her tiny body stiff and cold. But Erin knew she wasn't dead. She couldn't be.

"Maybe they took you from me too soon. You just weren't ready yet, were you?"

Erin was a mother now. She knew what she had to do. She gently unwrapped her baby and wiped the slippery, cottage-cheese-like coating from her body. Erin lifted her gown, feeling along her lower body until she found the incision. The numbness from the epidural had worn off, and just touching the stitches sent flashes of pain throughout her body.

She used her fingernail to rip at the stitches, clenching her teeth together so she couldn't cry out. She put her feet in the stirrups and braced herself. Blood poured from the wound as she opened it up. The stitches lay in a pile next to her, like dismembered spider legs. Blood and mucous dripped from her hand onto the clean bed. She wiped her hand on the sheets then gently turned her baby so that her feet were facing Erin.

She tried to curl Olivia into the fetal position, but the baby's stiff limbs wouldn't bend. Erin didn't want to break the baby's bones, so she gave up trying. *Olivia will curl up on her own once she's back where she should be.*

She held the incision apart with her right hand, feeling her skin rip as she tugged it open. She cried out in pain, but didn't stop. She thrust Olivia into the opening, feet first, feeling tiny toes pressing against her organs. She gasped in pain and stopped pushing Olivia, trying to catch her breath.

Erin wiped sweat away from her face with the back of her free hand. Blood streaked her face. Determined, she grabbed the baby with both hands and forced her up inside the incision.

Something ruptured inside her, but she didn't care, even though the pain was excruciating. She screamed, trying to get the baby to fit back into her womb. Her body could no longer accommodate Olivia. Erin yanked at her skin, widening the incision. Her skin tore, globs of yellow fat mixed with blood oozing from the gaping wet wound, plopping onto the floor beside the bed.

The tiny body, now bent and bruised, lay in the wide gap of her torso. Erin tugged on either side of the gash to close the incision, but the flesh slipped from her gore-covered hands. She fell back against the pillows, consciousness fading as her blood dripped onto the sleek white tiles.

Alec and the doctor burst into the room when they heard Erin scream. Alec vomited at the sight before him. Blood soaked the sheet under his wife. Her hands were bloody, too, as well as her face where she rubbed it. He dropped to his knees at the sight of Olivia's little head poking out of the hole in

Erin's stomach, lolling with the rise and fall of Erin's last breaths.

Erin smiled through the pain, her face pale and her eyes vacant.

With the last reserve of strength she had left, she whispered to her husband. "It's okay, Alec—it's going to be okay. She wasn't ready to be born yet. She just needs some more time inside me. Just a little more time."

ABOUT THE WRITERS

Ruth Anna Evans is a horror writer, anthologizer, and book cover designer who lives in the heart of all that is sinister: the American Midwest. She has self-published the horror collection *OH FUCK OH FUCK IT HURTS* and is the editor of *Ooze: Little Bursts of Body Horror*. She also wrote two spooky novellas, and medical horror novella, *Against Medical Advice*. Ruth Anna loves horror that hurts.

Candace Nola is a multiple award-winning

author, editor, and publisher. She writes poetry, horror, dark fantasy, and extreme horror content. She is the creator of Uncomfortably Dark Horror, which focuses primarily on promoting indie horror authors and small presses with weekly book reviews, interviews, and special features. Books include *Breach, Beyond the Breach, Hank Flynn, Bishop, Earth vs The Lava Spiders, The Unicorn Killer, Unmasked, The Vet, Desperate Wishes, Transformation, Zombie Ducks, Zippers* and many more. Her short stories can be found in *The Baker's Dozen* anthology, *Secondhand Creeps, American Cannibal, Just A Girl, The Horror Collection: Lost Edition, Exactly the Wrong Things* and many others.

Antonija Mežnarić is a Croatian writer and editor who lives and breathes speculative fiction. She writes queer horror and fantasy, mostly inspired by South Slavic folklore, which is evident in her folk horror collection *The Lost Treasure Hunters and Other Tales of Folk Terrors*, several published horror novellas, various short stories in anthologies and magazines, and the dark urban fantasy novel *From the Cradle to the Grave*. You can follow her book ramblings on <u>hauntednarratives.com</u> or on Instagram and TikTok @antonijamezni.

Nuno Gonçalves was born in Viana do Castelo, Portugal, in 1985. His love for reading fostered the desire to one day see his own words on paper, bound and waiting for a reader. However, he chose a different path, and Medicine drew him in more than literature. He is currently an ophthalmologist at the Hospital de Faro. In 2022, he embarked on a new journey in fiction writing. He has published short stories in anthologies by Grupo Editorial Divergência, including the story "O Óbolo de Caronte" in the anthology Des/pudor and "Eva" in the anthology In/sanidade. He was the Portuguese finalist in the EACWP microfiction competition on two occasions (2022 and 2023). In 2022, his first novel, *O Pacto*, won the António de Macedo Award. The same novel also earned him the Grande Prémio Adamastor de Literatura Fantástica Portuguesa in 2024 and became Divergência's best-selling book of 2024.

Marie Lestrange is a multipassionate badass that plays eight musical instruments and is deathly afraid of chickens. She's the author of gothic historical novels *Crimson Cobblestones* and *The Devil's Colony*. She hosts a weekly indie Horror podcast called Moths to the Flame. She's obsessed with research into the macabre, true crime, and occultish practices and is also the founding chairman of the Horror Writers Association Tennessee Chapter. When not writing, she and her writer husband, Bert, love traveling with their little Hobbit outside of the East Tennessee mountains they call home.

Rebecca Burgess is an avid indie horror reader/reviewer, and resides in Central Illinois with her husband, three children, and three dogs. Thankfully, she hasn't lived through all of the horrors she wrote about in this story, but quite a few aspects are written from previous experiences and fears throughout the beginning of her kids' lives. Whenever she has spare time, she loves to read, bake, and play games with her family. This is the first story she's written since she was a teenager and is very happy to pick back up in her favorite genre.

Peter J. Larrivee is a horror writer from the Land of Lovecraft, just a little South of Providence. He has four published books, and has had his stories featured on Trembling with Fear, in Perihelion, and various anthologies such as *Night Terrors Volume 23, Dead of Winter*, and *Hell is for Children*. He has also been a regular contributor to local arts and entertainment publication *Motif Magazine*.

Deborah Coldiron has loved all things spooky since she got ahold of *The Complete Works Of Edgar Allan Poe* in fourth grade. She is a veteran graphic designer, a ceramic artist, and a middle school teacher. Editor and designer of *Cooks of Horror* (the official Books of Horror author cookbook), Deb is also a writer of random short stories, including "Moon

Through the Pine Boughs" from RJ Roles' anthology *Season of the Witch*.

Patrícia Lameida grew up among books, adventures and new worlds. From an early age, she wrote poems and short stories that she forgot over time. Life diverged from the world of letters during her education and entry into the job market. She soon rediscovered this passion, maintaining a literary criticism blog for several years and writing short texts, some of which can be found in several anthologies.

Autumn Weese spends her days working at her local public library and her nights editing. She received her MA in English Literature from the University of Arkansas. Autumn is a fan of horror and mystery. In her free time, Autumn is usually watching scary movies or playing cozy video games. Often, she's doing both at the same time. She's a very proud aunt and pet-mom.

S.E. Howard has had several short stories

published in independent anthologies, including "You've Been Saved" in the 2020 vacation-themed *Worst Laid Plans* by Grindhouse Press. "You've Been Saved" was later adapted for the screen in the 2022 GenreBlast film anthology *Worst Laid Plans*. Additionally, she has a horror novella, *Prairie Madness* from Unveiling Nightmares, and two full-length horror novels under contract for publication through Wicked House Publishing.

Emma Rose Darcy emerged, fully formed, five years ago and slithered snakelike down from the mountains. She writes dark fantasy and horror. Emma suffers Basilar Migraine so sometimes real life is weirder than anything she could ever write. She stumbled upon horror, discovering authors like Joe Donnelly and G M Hague among the Kings and Rices in charity shop books cases. It may be why she has a hunger for reading and writing body horror and transformation horror stories, hauntings and huntings.

C.J. Subko is a dreamer and a dabbler. She has a Ph.D. in Clinical Psychology from Michigan State University and a B.A. in Psychology and English from the University of Notre Dame, which makes her highly qualified to think too much. Her short fiction publications include *Skin Anthology* (Bag of Bones press, June 2024), *Cold Signal* (September 2024), *Die Laughing* (October 2024), *Small Wonders* (November 2024), *Morgana le Fay* (Flame Tree Press; March 2025), and upcoming issues of *The Deadlands* and *Penumbric Speculative Fiction*. She is a member of the HWA. Her novels are represented by Maria Brannan at Greyhound Literary Agency. She can be found at www.cjsubko.com.

Jacy Morris is an Indigenous author. He is a registered member of the Confederated Tribes of Siletz. At the age of ten he was transplanted to Portland, Oregon, where he developed a love for punk rock and horror movies, both of which tend to find their way into his writing. He has been an English and social studies teacher in Portland, Oregon since 2005. He has written several novels, including the *This Rotten World* series, the *One Night Stand at the End of the World* series, and *The Enemies of Our Ancestors* series… and many more!

Amanda DeBord is a horror writer and editor. She has recent stories in *Phantasmagoria* magazine and the anthologies *Bound in Blood* and *They're Out to Get You, Volume One*. When she's not working, she spends her time trail running and building spooky dioramas in the woods. She lives in St. Louis with her husband, two children, and the ghosts of several cats.

Australian horror author Tory Favro pushes the boundaries of extreme horror from his home base in Geelong. His latest work, *Piñata* (2024), plunges readers into a disturbing tale of madness centered around a party in Apartment 4, cementing his reputation for unflinching, visceral storytelling. His earlier works include *Tin Man*, a pitch-black comedic reimagining of *The Wizard of Oz*, and the acclaimed *Little Death Books* series, which pairs haunting illustrations with adult horror narratives. His ongoing *An Other Earth Story* series, featuring *The Dead of Christmas* and *The Dead of Egypt*, continues to captivate readers with its unique blend of horror and alternate reality.

Paul Avery Tindol is a horror author from Center, Texas. He's been writing stories since he could pick up a pencil, and obsessed with all things spooky since his babysitter showed him *A Nightmare on Elm Street*. He is the author of *Hunting Snipe: and Other Notes on the East Texas Cattle Mutilations, This House Will Never Be Warm*, and many short stories that have been featured on podcasts like Creepy, NoSleep, and Someone Just Like You. He lives with his wife in Dallas, Texas and they are expecting their first child in April 2025.

Sheri White's stories have been published in many anthologies and zines, including an essay in the Notable Works for the HWA Mental Health Initiative, an essay in *JAKE*

Magazine, *Halldark Holidays* (edited by Gabino Iglesias), and The Horror Writers Association's *Don't Turn Out the Lights* (edited by Jonathan Maberry). Recent publications include *Crab Apple Literary*, *Litmora*, *voidspace zine*, and *Broken Antler Magazine*.

ALSO FROM RUTH ANNA EVANS

Novellas
What Did Not Die
Do Not Go in That House
Cargo
Against Medical Advice

Collections
OH FUCK OH FUCK IT HURTS:
A Collection of Medical Horror

No One Can Help You:
Tales of Lost Children and Other Nightmares

Anthologies
Dark Blooms:
Girls' Coming-of-Age Horrors
OOZE: Little Bursts of Body Horror